by A. LaFaye

Aladdin Paperbacks

New York London Toronto Sydney Singapore

First Aladdin Paperbacks edition June 2001

Aladdin Paperbacks
An imprint of Simon & Schuster Children's Publishing Division
1230 Avenue of the Americas
New York, NY 10020

The text for this book was set in Granjon.

Printed and bound in the United States of America

10 9 8 7 6 5 4 3 2 1

The Library of Congress has cataloged the hardcover edition
as follows:
LaFaye, A.
Edith Shay / by A. LaFaye.
p.   cm.
Summary: Leaving her home in Wisconsin in 1865, sixteen-year-old
Katherine sets out for Chicago to prove to her family that she can
make a life for herself.
ISBN 0-670-87598-8 (hc.)
[1. Self-reliance—Fiction. 2. United States—History—
1865–1898—Fiction.] I. Title PZ7.L1413Eg 1998 [Fic]—dc21
98-16832
CIP AC
ISBN 0-689-84228-7 (Aladdin pbk.)

The North Western Telegraph Co.

———————— ▬ ————————

Dated: __August 2, 1869__

Received at: __Clarkston Michigan Office__

To: __Mrs. Charles Roberts__

From: __Mrs. Albert Lunden__

Katherine arriving August 9.   Train
arrives 9:00 P.M.   Keep her waiting.
Will send money for return fare.

Candace

Wayward

My hands were addicted to ink. For as long as I can remember, I favored a good newspaper over maple syrup candy floating in a cup of cider, a cool dip in Miller's Creek on an egg-frying hot day, or even a trip to Madison. In my mind, the only rival to a good newspaper was a train headed out of Wisconsin. The truth was, trains and newspapers were my passions, and there was nothing I could do to get them out of my blood.

On Saturdays, my father shoveled coal to chip away at the balance of the note the bank had on our family for building a fancy plank house in the middle of Wisconsin logging country. While Father worked with the other men to fill the coal car, I kept my place on the bench beside the employee door. I watched people as they dribbled out of the train's stairwell with wrinkled clothing, wobbly knees, and pasty smiles to meet their hosts. When the last person staggered from the steps, I watched the windows to see the conductor pass through the train, looking left, then right, making sure nothing and no one but himself remained behind.

No matter who the conductor was, young or old, fat or thin, he would squint up to the sun and adjust to the bright light as he came down the steps. On the platform he'd stretch out his back, then check his watch. Conducting creates an obsession with time. Close to a hundred conductors stepped onto that platform in the ten years I haunted that bench. They all knew me by name. The man from Minneapolis with the eyebrows resembling misplaced mustaches always patted me on the head as if I was the dog he'd left at home. "Here you are, Katherine," he'd say as he handed me the paper. I liked the script on the *Star,* but the print was often smudged due to his sweaty hands.

One conductor I can recall right down to the Mason's pin on his collar was a man named Buford. I couldn't believe my ears when I heard the railroad was adding a connection to Chicago.

Seeing Buford made me a believer. I saw the newspaper tucked under his arm as he stepped off the train; it was almost as thick as a pound of sliced bacon, with far too many pages for a local paper. The letter cresting over his wrist was a *C*.

I inched to the edge of the bench and said, "Excuse me, sir?"

He stopped and tipped his hat to me. "Hello there, young lady. And what is your name?"

I stood right up and pulled out my skirts to smooth the wrinkles, "Katherine Lunden."

"Proper name. Mine's Buford Marks. Now, what are you doing sitting here all by your lonesome?"

"Waiting for a newspaper."

He laughed with the dry-needle crunch of an old man. "Now, what do you want with a paper?"

"To read it, sir."

"Read?" The laugh seemed to be swallowed by his expanding eyes. He tapped the paper under his arm. "You want to read this paper?"

"Yes, sir."

"What for?"

"Chicago's in there." I pointed.

"Aren't you a bit young to be traveling to Chicago?"

"Yes, sir. I just want to know more about it."

"All right then." He handed the paper to me. "Free of charge."

With that paper in hand, I could go anywhere in Chicago. From an advertisement for fresh fruit on the third page, I could walk to the market on the corner of Michigan and Third and buy apples for a penny apiece. There was once a full-page article about a museum exhibit on safari animals. By the end of it, I could see the hardwood floors polished to a shine, reflecting wavy images of the giant, stuffed beasts carried across continents.

Then again, given my mother's view on leaving home, I was lucky to be able to step outside my front door. She'd even objected to my job at the mercantile, changing window displays and restocking for Mrs. Bowfield. Mother felt I should be home keeping house as a good woman did. Since I had turned sixteen, she regarded me as a woman. It didn't make me feel all that womanly the way she had me scrubbing floors and chopping wood. A woman wore fine clothes and hosted tea socials in her parlor. We didn't even have a parlor.

The thought of my leaving made my mother rigid and silent. I guess maybe she knew I was raising money so I could make my way to

Chicago. She'd rather I married some Wisconsin farm boy and settle down. I longed to marry, too, but not some country boy. I wanted to marry a city gentleman who would treat me like a lady and take me to the far reaches of the country.

Mother finally asked me about my job when we took in our first harvest of apples. She was cutting apples for a pie, when I came in to help her with supper. Without looking up, she asked, "What does Mrs. Bowfield have you doing down at the store?"

Strapping on an apron, I said, "Unpacking the new merchandise."

Mother hummed one low note, then asked, "A lot of folks come in on Saturday, I suppose."

"Yes, it's nice to see everyone when they stop in for supplies," I said, taking an apple in hand to core it.

She nodded, and a smile crossed her lips. "You see any young men you fancy?"

"No," I answered honestly.

Her mouth slid into a frown. She cut up an entire apple before she spoke again. "Your aunt Fran asked for help with this year's harvest. I wrote to tell her you'd be glad to, and she was so delighted she sent you a ticket."

My fingers froze at the thought of actually stepping onto a train. I had watched hundreds come and go, but I never thought I could afford to sit in one of those cars with the cloth-covered seats and hanging lanterns. Since I had only a dollar eighty-five saved, Chicago was still out of my reach. But Michigan would bring me closer. At that moment, I thought Mother had given me her silent approval.

When I didn't speak, Mother continued without stopping her work. "It's nothing to be excited about, Katherine. It'll mean twenty-one hours on a train. Your aunt will expect you to work. And I mean work. It won't be nearly so easy as the showcase work you do at the store."

The train could have gone in circles for all I cared. I packed that night. I placed two dresses, undergarments, a hairbrush, and three newspapers into a satchel. The slumped-over cloth bag sat by the front door for over a week. My mother kept tight-lipped and dry-eyed right up to when she saw me off at the front door. Gripping my hand, she said, "Come back to me, Katherine."

I smiled, but I wanted to cry. "Come see me off," I said as I tugged her toward the front steps.

She shook her head. "My feet are planted on this land. I don't need to go." My mother only hinted it, but my father's farewell told me they were truly afraid I wouldn't return. He kissed me on the cheek, then sat down beside me.

"Grandma Margaret made you these." He held up three sandwiches wrapped in a towel— they were honey and brown sugar, knowing Grandma. Father slid them into my satchel. He sat down, then held my hand. When the conductor made the last call, Father stood up and said, "You keep your head about you, girl. This world's a lot bigger than you think."

If I'd had any sense of what I was leaving behind, I would have watched him as he left the train. At the time, all I could think of was that I was finally on my way out of Wisconsin.

The train wasn't what I expected. The seats were covered in scratchy wool; the floors were so beaten down that they were warped and splintery. The lanterns flickered and clanked as the train pulled out of the station. I didn't care; I was on my way. But only to Michigan.

I'd never been to Michigan, but I'd read Aunt Fran's letters. It was all trees, rolling hills, and little farming towns just like my own town of Maustone. I wanted libraries with more books in one room than Wisconsin had in an entire county. I longed for museums with bits and pieces from all around the world—a lion that stalked railroad men on the savannas of

Africa—butterflies that fluttered their wings on the branches of trees rooted in the banks of the Amazon River—mummies who'd slept among their earthly possessions longer than my kinfolk had walked this earth. I wanted to be where I could catch a glimpse of the whole world. Chicago was that place, but my family would have none of it. A city was no place for a fine young girl. I wanted Chicago and I was getting Clarkston, Michigan. It didn't seem like a fair trade.

Afraid I'd give in to Chicago's pull at my heart, my mother booked me on a winding, roundabout route to Michigan, keeping me counties away from that grand city at all times. I didn't reach Clarkston until after sunset on the second day. The narrow platform was crowded with people waiting for the train to arrive. I searched the crowd for Aunt Fran and Uncle Charles as we pulled in, but I didn't see them. Stepping off the train, I felt as if I could float. It was almost as if the rocking of the train had hollowed out my bones, and I would have risen up in the air like a feather if I hadn't had my satchel to weigh me down.

People slowly disappeared off the platform—some boarding the train, others collecting passengers then heading home, but there was no sign of Aunt Fran and Uncle Charles. The station was a hollow shell by the time the train engine cooled. I sat on a church pew reclaimed by the Pacific Northwestern Railroad. It still held the scratches and oil marks of its parish on the arm. I sat through another arrival and departure waiting for my relatives to arrive. The train whistles rattled the wavy glass in the windows.

When the second train left, I began to pace the floor and watch the dust gather in clouds around my feet. I quickly lost my patience and went to the ticket counter. The man behind it had veins in the pattern of red snowflakes on his cheeks. He smiled as I approached and they expanded. "Can I help you, miss?"

"Sir, is there another train from Wisconsin today? I think my relatives might believe I'm arriving on it."

"The arrival times are up there on the board." He pointed over my shoulder.

A man on the bench beside the window said, "Can't you read?"

I turned to face the board the clerk pointed to in order to keep myself from shouting, "Of course I can read!" I'd been reading since I was six.

It was just that I knew what I'd find on that

board. I'd see "Chicago" in bright white letters drawn in chalk and it'd be too much to resist. I'd have to go. To keep my mind off Chicago, I recited the names of the seventeen presidents of the United States with their terms of office and places of birth. I got to Springfield, Illinois, for Abraham Lincoln and I had to take those letters in. "Springfield" was right next to "Lansing" and "Chicago" was written in under "Detroit." The next train for Chicago left in less than an hour, and the fare was only a dollar seventy-five.

No. I couldn't go. Lundens didn't leave their home. By the time I was born, in 1853, the Lundens had lived in Wisconsin for so long our name appeared on local maps. The "Lunden Woods" were just above the dot representing Maustone. My great-great-grandfather had settled there as a trader before the American colonists declared victory at Yorktown. Grandpa Jacob grew up on the farm his grandfather had carved out of the rugged woods.

From the day I was born, I was told how I'd live in Wisconsin forever, marry an earth-loving man who would buy land adjoining ours. He and I would build our house and raise a family. Our children would marry local folk, settle down nearby, then raise their own families. That was the way things were done in the Lunden clan. It was like a family gospel no one questioned. I accepted my family's plans as simply the way things were, until newspapers put a crack in my isolated home and showed me there was a whole world out there and a million ways to live in it.

Thinking back on all the places I longed to see, I felt as if I was going to burst like a target-practice apple if I didn't buy that ticket. The coins tucked away in my pocket were enough to cover the fare. I could walk up to the ticket counter and slide those coins over to the ticket clerk with an open palm. The clerk would adjust his gold spectacles as he asked my destination with a voice that echoed in his flattened nose. "Chicago" would roll off my lips, and he'd nod with a smile. The ticket would be perfect; no wrinkles, no smudges in the fresh ink. I'd carry it to the platform without sweating. It would be crisp and flat when I handed it to the conductor and took my place on a velvet-covered seat.

The toll of the clock in the corner brought me back to the station in Michigan. I had to keep my mind on my duty. I thought perhaps my aunt had left a message. Maybe they knew they'd be late. I went back to the clerk. "Excuse me, do you have a message for Katherine Lunden?"

"No, miss. No messages. What seems to be the trouble?"

The man on the bench spoke up again, his gravelly voice scraping inside my ears, "She's not a traveler, that one. Nervous, I suspect."

Grandpa always said I've got a temper that boils quicker than water on a bonfire, and I was ready to push that nosy old man right into the flames. What did he know of my travels? I kept my eye on the clerk's rosy snowflakes. "My relatives are simply late. Four hours late."

"Perhaps they had trouble on the road. Do you need someone to take you in, miss?" the clerk asked.

The bench man stood up to say, "Young girl like you shouldn't be left to her own defense."

No stranger was going to tell me my needs. "Thank you, no," I said to the clerk, ignoring the other man altogether. I went back to the pew where I'd left my satchel.

My body was too tired to pace, but my muscles were too eager to keep still, so I sat down on the bench below the slate board and let my feet sway. The rush of skirts pulled my purse to the floor. I bent over my knees to pick it up and came face to face with a cracked leather suitcase tucked under the bench. The case carried the marks of great use. The brass clasps were tarnished brown. The handle had been replaced with braided strips of twine turned black with hand sweat and dirt. The studs that lined the seams scratched the floor as I pulled it forward. The tag read, "Edith Shay, 1919 Fillmore Lane, Richmond, Virginia."

I searched the room for a face that fit the name. I was the only woman present. A man sat on a stool in the corner cleaning out the grooves in his pocket watch with his thumbnail. The ticket clerk was conversing with the bench man, who wore a wool suit that blended into the browns of the wall paint as he leaned next to the ticket window.

I knocked the suitcase over. The bang as it hit the ground didn't even raise an eyebrow between the two men, so I carried it over to the shelf below the window. My hands sweated with guilt as I opened it. Inside, I found no clues. Nothing that would point me in the right direction to find the woman's destination in the Midwest. There were fourteen tiny packages wrapped in crisp, brown paper of various shapes and sizes. Beside them was a dark gray wool dress with black velvet trim, a low, round, gray hat kept firm by a circular pillow covered with pink satin, and a pair of smooth leather gloves that felt like the skin on Grandma Lunden's cheeks when I'd pinch them for color before Sunday church services.

The bench man stood up straight when I set the suitcase on the ledge of the ticket window. I ignored him and asked the clerk, "Did you see the woman who left this behind?" Obviously, they weren't as good as they pretended to be about taking care of the women in the station.

The clerk bit his lip to hold back the laugh that shivered in his stomach. "Miss, there are a hundred ladies who travel through here every day."

"Is there somewhere I could leave this for her?"

"To be truthful, I'd just take it home to my wife if you left it. Most people get halfway to the next city before they realize they've left something behind. By that time it's too late. I've never seen a person with enough money to buy a ticket back here that had a suitcase with a rope handle."

The bench man, nodded saying, "Take it home yourself, miss. You look like you could use a handout."

That was all it took. His comment made me pull the suitcase back. It knocked into my knees.

They buckled, but I stood my ground. I wanted to tell them I'd sewn the dress I was wearing with my own two hands out of fabric that came from the store I helped stock, but then I thought I'd only be adding to his insult, so I decided to show him just what I could do on my own.

I pulled out the pine-green coin purse my father had given me and paid for a ticket to Chicago with the money I had saved up from working at the store. I was on the train with the suitcase in my lap before I realized what I had done. It was wrong to take another woman's suitcase. Even worse to abandon Aunt Fran without so much as a note to explain my whereabouts.

It didn't take a minute, after I slid the suitcase and my satchel under my feet, to prove that the bench man was right. There wasn't a woman in sight who didn't have a hat on her head and gloves on her hands. There wasn't a single dress that didn't have trim or ribbons. They wore dignified colors like cat gray and burgundy, as I sat in my plain, cornflower blue dress that barely touched the top of my shoes.

I sank into my seat in shame. With only ten cents to my name, I was riding toward a city that I knew by heart in print, but had never seen.

My ticket was soaked with sweat, and the

conductor stared at me when I handed it to him. "Are you traveling alone, Miss?"

"Yes, sir."

Shaking his head, the conductor walked away, his watch fob rattling. I thought he was just old-fashioned. Women could do quite well on their own. A man need not lead them everywhere. What was going to happen to me on a train, anyway?

The excitement of going to Chicago put Wisconsin far behind me. I could see the city in my mind. The wide streets where two wagons could pass each other with room to spare for a horse—or a celeripede. I'd seen an advertisement for one of these two-wheeled bone shakers. How I longed to try one—wheel my way around the pond in Humboldt Park, past the ladies with their parasols, the gentlemen with tailored suits and walking canes. I'd seen the beautiful park in real estate advertisements for the Humboldt Park neighborhood, which had a depot for the Chicago Pacific railroads, the park, the Powell Hotel, and even walks made of concrete so smooth you could iron fabric over them.

I had newspapers to thank for all my ideas of Chicago—and everywhere else, for that matter. My mother couldn't abide my love for print.

When I was a child, she told me I should find a better pursuit than filthy newspapers. By the time I was twelve, she wouldn't hear a word out of a newspaper. We were in the thick of the war with the South. The threat of the Rebels filled every page. With the drawn pictures of men crouched low on the battlefield and the words surrounding them, I could smell the blood and smoke, hear the screams and explosions. Father said the stories scared Mother.

When he came home from the logging camp each night, he called me over to the fireplace. I sat at his feet and read to the rest of the family, while Mother prepared the evening meal. I remember the shadows of the flames behind me dancing over the page.

For me, the Civil War wasn't a battle waged between two sides over a cause. It was something recreated in thin line drawings and printed words that fed a teasing fire in my heart. I was excited when headlines declared the end of another bloody battle not because it was over but because I could take in all the details one by one and bring them home to read in front of my family. I thought of myself as the Lundens' link to the rest of the world. And the fire inside me was a growing desire to see the world outside of Wisconsin.

My mother made it her duty to try to douse that fire. I remember a night in early March when she told me to help her wash the dishes. She didn't even look up from the bowl she was drying when she up and said, "I know you well enough to put your skin on and fool the Lord himself. I know you have your eye on living in a city. You can't wait to pack your bags and find yourself in Chicago."

"Why not, Mother? Think of all the places there, museums, libraries, and curio shops."

"And what do you need all that for, Katherine? You have a family right here; a house your father slaved for. You have no right to leave it."

"I'm not going to live here forever. I'll be married someday."

"Wisconsin's been this family's home since they came to this country. I see no reason why it can't be yours, too. For life."

Her standard speech sounded like a bad sermon. She delivered it whenever Thomas or I talked about going with Father on his annual trip to visit relatives in Mankato, Minnesota. Her connection with Wisconsin made it a sin for her to even talk about other states. Her sister Fran had committed the greatest sin by leaving the state entirely and settling on a Michigan cherry orchard with her husband, Charles.

I had to ask her, "Don't you ever want to see what's out there? To know what lies beyond Wisconsin?"

"Outside Wisconsin?" She bit her lip, chewing her thoughts before spitting them out. "I've seen what's outside Wisconsin. My father worked himself to death in a Virginia coal mine; turned him black inside and out. He came home on holidays coughing up bits of coal into his handkerchief. All he could talk about was coming home with enough money to move into our own house. His last letter said he would settle for being home, in Wisconsin, under any roof where he could rest. He was put to rest, all right. Six feet underground in our family plot." She pointed at me and I shivered. "Don't ever try and tempt me with places outside Wisconsin, Katherine. This is my home. It's where I belong. And you'd consider it your home, too, if you had the good sense God gave you."

I'd thought I could wear my mother down, show her over time how wonderful Chicago was. But the world conspired against me, flinging something horrible my way to crush my love of newspapers. The first blow came when my reading performances ended on April 21, 1865. It took a week for the news to travel west on the

Burlington line through Chicago. I stood in the doorway with the paper rattling in my hands as I fought to catch my breath. The whole household stopped to listen as I read the report of Abraham Lincoln's last hours. After weeks of disturbing dreams about his own death, President Lincoln had gone to see *My American Cousin* at Ford's Theatre just five short days after General Lee had surrendered. During the third act, the actor John Wilkes Booth burst into the president's box with a knife and a derringer to shoot the president in the head before jumping to the stage to make his escape. It was almost too unreal to believe. Reading the article made me feel hollow right down to the tips of my fingers.

No one spoke as I turned the paper down to see their reaction. My mother stood at the stove as the pot she had been stirring boiled over. Grandpa and Grandma sat on the bench below the window in the sitting room, their hands locked together so tight their knuckles whitened. My father walked up the stairs and didn't come down until supper. Thomas and I went outside to read the article again. We couldn't believe a man could charge out of a play and shoot the president.

The following Saturday, Father told me to keep my paper to myself for reading practice

before bed. Any word I spoke at the dinner table
was silenced by a stare. I suppose they believed
the bad news would never have come if I had not
read it out loud. But I knew different. I'd been
reading about the little children who lost their
hands to the churning looms of the textile mills,
the entire families swallowed by flames in tene-
ment fires, and the bent wreckage after trains
collided, since I was a child. The newspaper was
filled with those horrors, but I had always
thought they happened far off and over there.
They were the freak accidents that would never
happen to me. I overlooked them, forced myself
to forget them and turned instead to the beautiful descriptions of gala balls and museum
exhibits. Those were the things of the world that
I wanted to see.

My family wanted nothing of the outside
world, and I was drawn to it as if my soul had
been set adrift and I had to follow it, but no one
had understood. They all thought I was simply
lost in my own daydreams. But now here I was
riding across the Illinois prairie, and I'd be in
Chicago in no time. No time at all. The thought
of it made my insides turn to ice. I'd be there by
early evening, and there was so much to do. If
only I hadn't been so foolish with my money. I'd

purchased the fabric for my dress, the satchel for my things, and enough lemon drops to rot my teeth. I only had ten cents. What could I do in Chicago with ten cents? I'd have to find a place to stay. A job.

I would need to find a job that offered room and board along with a decent wage. I could cook, or sew, perhaps stock shelves in a store. In no time at all I'd have enough money for a fine dress, perhaps my own apartment with lace curtains and a window overlooking a park. I had all my plans laid out as I drifted off to sleep. Chicago would be the land the newspapers had always promised it to be.

Lessons

———▶✦◀———

It was the conductor who snapped me out of my stupor as he strolled down the aisle chanting, "Chicago next stop. Next stop, Chicago."

I was the first one to the door when the train lurched to a stop. The station was filled with so many people I thought I'd stepped right into the farming exhibits at the Juneau County Fair. The smells and sounds told me different. The musty stench of burnt coal mixed with sweat came into full contact with the camouflages of perfume, wax, and flowers.

I could see wilted floral displays crowded onto shelves in a tiny room of rough-hewed planks. Flowers cut to the quick and sold indoors? The thought had never entered my mind, but people seemed to enjoy stopping to take in the smell of the blossoms. A man picked out a bouquet of daisies as I stood there watching.

The station was not a fair. The people weren't smiling and searching their surroundings. They kept their eyes focused on their paths, their arms crossed over whatever they carried. The printed advertisements pasted onto the walls didn't draw their attention. They passed stores filled with books without a glance. No one nodded to a passerby with a smile of recognition. A voice carried over the hum of shuffling feet, flowing skirts, and mumbling chatter pulled my eyes into short focus. "Hot off the press! Get your evening edition!"

Hot ink. I could feel it against my hands as I fought through elbows, trench coats, and feather-plumed hats to reach the young boy clearing a path with the wooden box strapped over his shoulder, filled with newspapers. For five cents, I had the Chicago I'd always known.

Chicago by paper is a city of words and pictures carefully laid out by the typesetter. I could read them in any order or ignore them if I wanted to. I read three pages on a bench in a park before the real city pushed the words aside, dashing them apart with the distant clanging of a steeple bell. The jingle-clipping combination of carriages cut into the distant sounds of speech as they passed couples on the street. Above all these things was a hint of the familiar: the smell of water drifting in from a darkness beyond. The gas lamps lined the streets, hovering to meet the dry stench of cattle, their waste, dirt, and sweat.

I'd set my mind on the idea that I would go to the nearest telegraph office and wire my parents to beg for their help, until I recalled something my brother Thomas had once said when I was reading out of the Chicago paper. We were fishing off the bridge over the Wabash River, when he shook his pole over my paper to get my attention. "You aren't learning a thing from those papers, Riney. You mark my words. You'll step out into that big city of Chicago and it'll eat you up raw. You remember Gary Simons? He was all set on being a newspaperman in Chicago. He came back jumpier than a barn cat from all the pressures in the big city. Any time he heard a tea kettle blow, he near about jumped right out of his britches, because he'd rented himself a room by the train station and didn't get a wink of sleep with all them whistles blowing."

I'd promised Thomas then and there that I would show him just what I could do in Chicago. Remembering that oath turned me full around to thinking about how I could make my way in the city. When I stood up from that park bench, I was determined to prove Thomas wrong. My plan was to make enough money to have myself one of those apartments they rent out of the paper.

I'd talked to Mrs. Bowfield about them. They were tiny houses all built into one building. She'd lived in one when her husband, Edward, was the foreman of the shipping crew in the Madison branch of the Union Pacific. I would rent one of my own and invite my parents down to see a real city.

My first thought was to find a place to stay. I wandered through shadowy streets, avoiding the saloons I passed, until I came upon a lighted window where there were no men gambling or shouting about the glories of drink. The sign painted on the glass read, THE REST STOP HOTEL. Inside, a man stood behind a high wooden counter poring over an open ledger book. He looked up when I walked in, but he glanced over my shoulder when I stepped up to the counter as if he expected someone to be following me.

"May I have a room for the night?" I asked, as his brow wrinkled in confusion.

"What's that?" he asked. "Isn't there anyone with you, miss?"

"No, sir."

"I don't rent those kind of rooms."

"Excuse me, sir?"

"You should be ashamed of yourself, girl. You can't be more than fifteen."

"I'm sixteen, and I just want a place to sleep for the night."

"I can't be giving my paying guests any ideas. You should find yourself a church that will take you in."

"I've never been in this city before. I don't know where the churches are."

"Mary Sue?" he shouted over his shoulder toward an open door.

A woman emerged from the door wiping her hands on her apron, "Yes, Virgil?"

"This girl wants a room for the night."

Mary Sue reacted as if someone had poured cold water down her back. "Not in our hotel."

"I know that!" Virgil snapped. "Don't be telling me my business. I asked you out here to see if you had any work in the back."

"Have those sheets that need to be mended."

My fingers were numb from working a needle through torn cotton by the time I was shown to a room behind the main staircase, filled with odds and ends for the general upkeep of a hotel. Mary Sue handed me a blanket and pointed to the barren floor between a mop bucket and a pile of used pillows. "You can bed there for tonight, but you'd best be gone by morning before the guests get up and see you lurking in the halls."

Lying on that floor, the smell of dust almost choking me, I longed for home. I could see our place as it looked from the road. Pine trees fenced in the house with overlapping boughs that reached up to support the clouds. We lived in a two-story plank house nestled deep in the woods north of Maustone, Wisconsin. Built with money from years of railroad work, the house with the pale pine board walls and the rippled, store-bought glass in the windows held the pride of two generations of the Lunden family.

We kept that house so clean, you'd have to go to the barn to find any dust. Footsteps sounded crisp and clean on the wooden floors. They weren't covered with any fancy polish, but I loved the low echo of my father's footsteps as he walked from the front door to the back and blew out the lanterns on each porch. I could hear it from my bed upstairs, warm under the quilts Grandma Margaret had made. Thomas was usually snoring from the other side of the room. He could fall asleep as he undressed. Most nights, he fell asleep with one sock on, the other still clutched in his hand.

The next night I found myself washing dishes for a party of fifteen in a boardinghouse near the pier. It was plain to see that in order to have a place to stay for the night and a meal, I had to enter a hotel from the back door and ask if there was any work to be done. When the assigned duties were completed, there was usually a place to bed down tucked away from the view of the guests.

After sixteen years in the same bed, listening to Thomas with his dragging little snore, I felt so tiny and alone in a strange bed. After a few days, I wanted nothing more than to be in a familiar bed with sounds I knew chirping in the night. I longed for pine needles scraping the window in a small breeze or the creak of the back door as Grandpa Jacob sneaked out to the outhouse, but I couldn't run home like a lost child. I had to face Chicago and beat it. To do that, I had to find steady work and a permanent place to stay.

By luck or providence, I passed a restaurant looking for hired help one morning. It was called the Sunshine Cafe, but from the looks on

the faces inside, no one was serving any sunlight. Men crowded the tables, their shoulders
stooped, their faces bent down to their plates.
Most of them didn't even look at their neighbors
as they shoveled food into their mouths. The
black dust that covered them from their hair to
their boots told me they probably worked in the
coal refinery a few blocks off that filled the sky
above it with ebony clouds.

I saw an old man coughing over his soup, a
gray handkerchief to his mouth, and for a second he was my Grandpa Vince. My heart sank in
my chest and I grieved for my grandpa and that
old man, but only for an instant. The restaurant
owner came bustling out of the kitchen with
three plates clutched in each hand, shouting, "If
you're here for the waitress job, get your backside into the kitchen."

I rushed into the kitchen before I had time to
think. The cook was thinner than a dress on a
sewing form, and she worked in silence as she
pulled me into the pantry and trussed up my
hair. The apron she gave me went past the hem
of my dress. She pulled it out in front to hide the
fact that my chest was near to as flat as her stomach. To finish her transformation, she rubbed
my cheeks with paprika.

I laughed at the thought, and she shook her

finger in my face. "Hush child, this is what will make the difference between you making money and making babies for one of those hooting pigs you'll be waiting on. Keep your ankles out of their sight. Keep your personal goods to yourself, and let them think you haven't got the slightest idea about cooking." She stepped out of the pantry. "Besides, with the way you stink, I had to give you a little something to cut the edge. Don't want them running out of here without eating first."

I never learned the cook's name, and though I should have, I never got the chance to thank her. I dropped a plate of mashed potatoes covered with hot gravy into a man's lap because he told me I looked "fresh," then pinched me on the bottom. I lost all control of my hands. The owner sent me out the front door with a nickel to my name.

I soon discovered that the list of services a young woman could perform without training was quite short. I could be a maid if I knew how to clean properly, a cook if I could figure out how to keep from burning the food, a waitress, if I learned to control my reactions to pinching customers, a school teacher if I had a teaching certificate or even an inkling of how a schoolhouse was run, a nanny if I could find someone

31

who was willing to take me in without knowing my family and their roots, a milliner if I'd known the first thing about hats.

There was one skill I had that I didn't need to copy from others, and that was sewing. With this asset in my favor, I set out to find a seamstress in need of an assistant. I saw an advertisement in a discarded Sunday paper for blankets embroidered with hotel logos. Any shop that was seeking orders for hotel linens in Chicago was in need of help, or so I thought. I followed the address in the advertisement to a small shop three blocks off Ashland Avenue on Kilpatrick. It was "O'Dell's Royal Stitchery" by name, but there was nothing uncommon about it. Despite the bright green letters painted across the pine placard over the front of the building, it didn't distinguish itself from the storefronts that surrounded it. The brick walls were just as coalsoaked, the multipaned windows had as many tiny cracks, and the door held all the same marks of customers coming and going with packages in hand and places to go.

I stepped inside with the paper held under my arm and Edith's suitcase in my hand. The front room was marked by the stenciled pattern of the window frames as the midafternoon sun drenched the floor with light. A woman stood at the counter sharpening needles. A leather thimble covered her index finger as she worked.

"Good afternoon," I said to her from the door.

She looked up, the smile on her face that pushed out her hollow cheeks melting when she focused on me. "Can I help you?"

"I was looking for work?"

"Did you sew that?" She pointed to my dress with the needle she was sharpening.

It felt like her question shrunk my dress right on my body. "Yes," I admitted.

"Aeslynn will never hire you." She bowed to her work before adding, "Check down the street with Fentner's. They can always use someone to hem trousers."

A woman emerged from the back room. The thick brilliance of her black hair drew all my attention. "What is it that I won't be doing?" Her voice was a high, chippering, accented sound. I learned later that it was a lifetime in Ireland that put the twitter in her voice.

"This girl here wants a job." The woman at the counter nodded in my direction.

Aeslynn moved around the counter to have a full view of me and granted me the same of her. Her dress was made of a dark blue taffeta with a high shine. "Well, put that suitcase down so I can have a look at you." She seemed to struggle with her lips to get them to form the sounds she wanted to hear. I complied, and she examined me with her lips pursed and her dark eyebrows pushed down over her pale blue eyes. "It's the dress she doesn't like, lass. Elly here doesn't like anything in blue, says it's the sign of a weak character." Aeslynn stepped closer and whispered, "Shows that she hasn't been in Ireland. We treasure our blue. Only the good families have blue in their tartan.

"You can sew, can you?" Aeslynn bent toward the hem of my dress. Her voice had a rhythm all its own. The way it flowed out of her mouth made it sound as if she was trying hard not to sing. "Can I have a look?"

I nodded and she picked up the fabric in her hand. She ran her fingers over the seam, then pulled at the thread. "Learn sewing from your mother, did you?"

"Yes, ma'am."

"She sew all your clothes?" With a passing glance at the suitcase, she stood up straight.

"I do."

"Well Edith, how much are you willing to learn?" Aeslynn tilted her head back to look at me along the slope of her thin, pointed nose.

"Edith?"

"That's what it says on your case there. Would

you prefer Miss Shay? You don't look the formal type."

I felt a bit guilty for stealing the name from the real Edith, but it felt good somehow. Like a new beginning. "No, Edith is fine, and I'd like to learn as much as I can."

"Good, because with your talent, I wouldn't trust you to mend my sheets." She walked around the counter with her back facing me. "You start Monday at six A.M. A minute late and I give the job to the next fresh lass to walk through that door."

"Thank you, ma'am." I nodded to her back as she walked around the counter. "Thank you. I'll be here on time," I blurted as I stepped backward out the door.

"That you better, if you want to learn how to sew," Aeslynn said with a smile.

A job only solved half my problem. I still needed a place to stay, and the job didn't start for three days. I was forced to return to the back doors of hotels. I was refused at four different places before I knocked on the service entrance of the Greymore on State Street.

"Who in the Sam Hill's pounding back here?" A young man in a gray waistcoat with silver buttons leaned out the back door. He looked me over with a furrow in his brow. "And what do you want?"

"I was wondering if you had any work for a room."

He laughed, and I knew I'd stumbled over another invisible rule. "Here?" he shouted. "Young lady, this isn't a bed and breakfast. You're at a fifty-room hotel asking for a hand-out."

I had no idea that there was any connection between the number of rooms and the options for room and board, so I was unable to respond. He stepped into the alley and let the door close behind him. "Look, if you need a place to stay, you can apply for the overnight cook position. They'll give you a room, and you just answer room service calls."

Room service was another foreign concept that slipped by me, but the room was an answer to my problem, so I agreed. "Any suggestions on how I can get this job?"

"First off, I'd leave that suitcase behind or they'll think you're a runaway."

"What?" I asked looking down at Edith Shay's travel-worn suitcase with my own satchel tucked inside.

"It looks like you've come a thousand miles with no one to look after you." That was close to the truth, but I was beginning to see his point. If they suspected me as a runaway they'd never hire me for fear my parents would come looking for their daughter and cause trouble when they found me.

"Where can I leave it?"

"I'll sneak it in for you."

"Thank you." I gave it away without question.

"Can you read?"

"Yes."

"How's your cooking?"

"I'm quite—"

"Doesn't matter. If you can fill out the application form and you don't complain about the job requirements, you'll get it. I'll introduce you to Mrs. Hessmueller; she's in charge of the kitchen staff."

Mrs. Hessmueller had as much spit and hissing in her personality as there was in saying her name. I quickly assumed that the extra-wide doors of the Greymore were designed for her huge body. All the weight that wrinkled over her joints stretched her patience to the breaking point. A blank look was enough to send her into a rage.

Her similarities to the newspaper caricature of Stephen Douglas turned out to weigh in my favor. I had to keep a tight-lipped smile all the while she was explaining the position, to hold back my laughter, and she thought I was pleased with the job description. "I'll warn you here and now," she sucked air in through the gap in her teeth to punctuate her sentence, "this is not a walk in the park. Any guest at any hour can order any dish. You are to be out of your bed and into this kitchen before the service bell tolls three times. No order should take more than half an hour to prepare. If a guest complains that he had to wait more than that for an order, you'll be on the street. Understand?"

I nodded, and she stepped through the side door of the kitchen into a dim hallway. "This is your room." She opened the door and I followed her to have a look.

Visions of a horse stall filled my head as I stared into the cramped space stuffed with a cast-iron bed and a washstand. I think it was the hay sticking out of the mattress that made me imagine a barn. My mother's voice drowned out Mrs. Hessmueller's description of the room's generous features: "Beggars cannot be choosers."

I took the job and started that night. One of the dinner cooks gave me a tour of the hotel, with particular attention paid to the kitchen and its contents. When she showed me the pantry, she stuck her fingertip into the top of the candles to see if they'd melted in the heat of the day. She made me think of Grandma Margaret, who was always worried about melted wax getting on the sewing she kept stored under the candles.

Through the cook's entire tour of the upper floors of the hotel, I was back in Wisconsin thinking of Grandma embroidering flower petals. I didn't return to Chicago until the door snapped shut behind her. I went straight to my room to try writing a letter to my family. The young man in the gray waistcoat knocked at my door only minutes after I closed it.

"Here's your suitcase." I took it from him and slid it under the bed. "Well, good luck." He turned to leave.

"Wait. I'd like to thank you for all your help."

"Don't bother. You seem like a pretty nice girl." He nodded as he backed out the hallway. "Have a good night and don't let them Grangers make any advances on you."

I took his advice with a smile, then went straight to bed. To my surprise, the bed was comfortable, but I rarely slept in it. There was a Grange convention in the hotel for the week-end, and I was out of bed what seemed like a thousand times to prepare the cravings of every hotel guest. When I took the job, I never thought I would have any trouble knowing how to cook the things the guests asked for, but when a man ordered hominy grits, I knew I was standing in a hole I would have to work myself out of. Luckily, the man who ordered it was kind enough to explain that they were a grain, much like oats boiled and served with butter, plenty of pepper, and bacon grease.

By Sunday evening, the tick of the clock gave me an itch under my skin. Boiled down to the bone by the whole ordeal, I was out of bed as soon as I heard a guest step into the hall above my bed where the bell cord hung. The bell hadn't tolled more than twice by the time I was at the top of the stairs with a pencil and paper in my hand. With the order taken, I had to prepare whatever their stomachs desired. It could be steak or chicken. Some men even wanted an entire meal at two o'clock in the morning. To complete this job, I had to sleep in my clothes and stoke the fire hourly. I tried to put in enough wood to keep it going for several hours on Friday night, but it got so hot, I nearly started the towel on fire when I opened the oven. From the moment the dinner cooks hung their aprons on the hooks by the door for the evening until sunrise, I was running an endless race against time. I tried to sleep during the day, but the commotion in the kitchen was enough to make me think I was sleeping in a train depot.

On Monday, I met the early morning cook on my way out the door. I was at the doorstep of the Royal Stitchery with bags under my eyes and Edith Shay's suitcase in my hand at 6:00 A.M. by the toll of the clock in the church a block away. Aeslynn was smiling as she opened the door. But as she saw my sorry state she said, "Heavens! What on earth have you been doing?"

"I have a cooking job at the Greymore," I explained, stepping inside.

"Then what are you doing here?"

"I needed the job at the Greymore for a place to stay."

"Stay?" She shook her head in confusion. "You mean your family doesn't live here in Chicago?"

"No, ma'am."

"You aren't no runaway, are you?" She leaned her head back to examine me over her nose. "Don't lie to me now."

"N–o." I stuttered, mostly because I didn't quite know the answer to her question. Had I run away? I suppose I had. I hadn't exactly left home with my parents' blessing. Were they looking for me? I closed my eyes and held my breath. I didn't want to think about it. I promised myself I'd write to my parents as soon as I had a spare minute, so they wouldn't have to worry about me anymore.

Aeslynn ran her eyes over me to test my answer, then said, "I won't have none of my employees working themselves to the bone for a few quid. You can take the room above the shop if you clean up after the others leave and open up in the mornings. Send that Greymore business to its grave where it belongs."

"Thank you, ma'am." I thanked the Lord for giving me such a generous woman for my first real boss. In just two meetings, Aeslynn made me feel as if I really could make my way in Chicago.

"Put your suitcase to the wall over there and have a seat next to Elly. Watch what she does and learn." Aeslynn disappeared into the back room.

One of the women across the room whispered to the other, "This is the first time I've seen Mrs. O'Dell here at the crack of dawn."

"Don't say another word," Elly said under her breath. She was sitting at one of two long wooden tables behind the service counter sewing a hidden hem into a set of curtains. I took a seat next to her.

I tried to watch in earnest, but the room attracted my attention more than fabric and thread. The only light came from the front window, and it didn't reach into the corners of the oblong room of plank walls. The walls in my own house would have been destined to fade to the same shade of dull gray. I finally understood why my mother was so insistent on painting the walls with pitch every two years.

Two women who shared the other table sat on the same bench, their shoulders only a few inches apart as they leaned over another set of curtains from the same fabric. "That's Louise and Opal Dyer. They married brothers," Elly said without looking up.

"Their own?"

"No, fool." Elly scowled. "Louise was courted by a man, and his brother decided to court Opal. They got married on the same day. I think they'd live in the same house if they could."

"Oh," was all I could manage to say. I wasn't really that stupid, I just was too nervous to think straight. From the Dyer sisters, my eyes wandered along the wall papered with yellowing advertisements from the *Tribune*. Through the doorway next to the counter, I could see into the back room where Aeslynn sat stiffly in a chair, her hands pressed into folds of cloth on a tiny table crowded with some black iron contraption. I saw her knee rise up under her skirts, and the room filled with a low growl. "What's that?" The machine started sucking up the cloth and spitting it back out on the other side of the table.

"That's a sewing machine."

"Really?" I leaned closer. I'd seen them advertised in newspapers, but I'd never been this close to an actual machine.

Elly shook her head. "You'd better keep your eyes on this hem or Aeslynn will sew it to your forehead."

Elly made Aeslynn sound fierce, but she was exactly the type of woman I wanted to be. Everything she said was a declaration. She never lowered her head. Her eyes were looking straight ahead when she walked; people smiled when she passed them. Her clothes were more elegant than those I'd seen in advertisements. There was never less than seven yards of fabric surrounding her in crisp waves as she walked. Bows, ribbons, ruffles decorated each new dress. When she tired of one, she'd sell it and make another. She sewed them all on the whirring machine designed by a Mr. Singer.

As the hours passed, I found myself staring at

her while she worked at that whirring machine. She had her back toward me, elbows out, guiding the fabric. It took me a while, but then I realized I was seeing my mother when I looked at Mrs. O'Dell.

Even more than her face, I recalled the pear shape of my mother's shoulders jutting up and down as she kneaded bread. I would watch her from the table, her hands floating from bowl to flour sack, creating small clouds just above the counter. They would jump out for soda and cinnamon, but her elbows never moved. Everything had to be in its place. Flour on her left, then soda, then cinnamon, then butter, then milk.

A word rarely left her lips when she cooked. She had what she wanted where she wanted it; heaven forbid it should be moved. If her hand shot out for cinnamon and didn't find it, she'd bend her shoulders back, then turn on her heels. Her eyes would search slowly, as if they hadn't moved in a while and didn't know quite what they were doing. If they didn't settle on the object, she'd yell, "Where on God's green earth has my cinnamon been carried off to?"

If someone didn't tell her in a matter of minutes, supper was served cold. Everyone would be seated at the table. Father's hands were folded for grace, his bright red, bristly eyebrows pulled tight to hide the frustration in his eyes. Mother sat with her back to the stove as we watched steam rise off the food. No one talked. Thomas twisted a napkin around his hands to keep from grabbing a slice of hot bread from the edge of the stove just above his shoulder. Grandpa kept his eyes trained on Father in a way that asked, "How can you let a woman run you like that?" Grandma kept straight in her chair with her eyes fixed on my mother. She didn't approve of a woman who kept food from her family.

When she was sure the heaviness of waiting was thick upon our tongues, Mother served food to Father.

The truth of the matter was, Mrs. O'Dell was nothing like my mother or me. She had never had to enter a hotel kitchen to work for a night's rest. Her home was a house all to itself in the new community of Lake Forest just outside Chicago. Her husband, an Irishman from Dublin, drove her to work each morning in their two-horse buggy.

When I saw him that first Tuesday morning, I was frozen in place like a mannequin in the window of a department store. He wore an ash-gray top hat and a deep blue ascot, but it wasn't his appearance that made me like him so. He stood beside the carriage and held his hand up to help his wife down. He didn't grab her by the waist and hoist her out like a sack of potatoes the way my father used to do with me. Aeslynn put her hand in his and they smiled at each other and laughed. She probably told him a joke.

As he opened the door for her, he said, "Right then, Aeslynn, see you when the chickens go to roost." He kissed her on the cheek.

"Have a fine day, Ethane," Aeslynn said.

"Aye, you too." He tipped his hat as he passed in front of a woman walking by.

A man who called his wife by her first name, even in front of strangers. My father called my mother just that, "Mother." It was as if he thought of her more as a mother to his children than a wife. Father told me once that he called her "Miss Cavanagh" when they were courting. It wouldn't have been proper to call her "Candace." Sometimes it seemed like being proper meant slipping so far inside yourself you disappeared. A Candace became "Mother." Losing my own name and becoming just a title would have made me feel so lonely. Mr. O'Dell knew when to be proper. He dressed so finely, helped his wife from the carriage, and tipped his hat to strangers, but he called his wife by her first name to show how close he felt to her.

Indeed, Mr. O'Dell was the type of man I wanted to marry. So kind and well-respected. When he walked into the shop, the patrons stepped aside to let him pass, and inquired about his business as a lawyer in loud voices filled with respect. Aeslynn said he was only a junior partner in a firm with fourteen names on the door, but his superiors promised him that his day in court would come. He certainly had the skill and grace to argue any case.

Beyond showing me, with the patience of her patron saint, Cecilia, how to sew, Aeslynn gave me the first piece of Chicago that matched my dreams. That room above the shop fit my idea of a Chicago room right down to the view of the towering buildings on State Street. The bed was wide enough for two, and the mattress was filled with cotton. I had a wardrobe to myself. A nightstand stood by my bed with a glass pitcher and bowl instead of tin ones. I could take thirteen steps from the end of the bed to the door. It was mine. That night after I closed the shop, I danced a little jig just to prove that I had enough room to do it in.

I was so happy, I collapsed onto the bed with

laughter. From there, I could see out the window. Across the way was a cobbler's shop, and his family had their room above it. I could see the soft glow of a lamp through the curtains in one of the windows. It made me think of the lantern my father carried on his way home from the logging camp.

Every night back home, I went to the window next to the front door and kept watch for Grandpa Jacob and Father. As loggers, they worked until sundown. I couldn't see a thing outside the window unless I pressed my face up against the cold, rippled glass and cupped my hands around my eyes to keep out the light from the kitchen.

In the moonlight, the road was filled with shadows, and I couldn't tell a person from a tree until the lantern lights appeared on the hill north of our house. They looked like two balls of fire hovering over the road. Grandpa and Father walked home with David Gayle, the town fiddler. They parted ways at Malhoney Road. Mr. Gayle would flash his lantern to say hello to me, because he knew I watched from the window. Then his lantern light would disappear into the trees.

After leaving Mr. Gayle, Grandpa and Father

moved on. As they got closer to the house, I
could see their walking feet in the swaying light
from the lantern. I was the first to tell Mother
when they needed patchwork done on their
boots.

Grandpa hung the lantern outside the door
and blew it out to avoid attracting bugs.
Thomas lived for the nights when Grandpa
Jacob forgot to snuff out the lamp. He'd sit on
the front stoop and wait for moths to flutter up
to the light, then pull up the glass and blow
them right into the wick. He'd get all giggly
when he saw the veins in their fragile wings lit
up in flames. I thought it was a terrible thing for
him to do, but I'd be a liar if I didn't admit I was
fascinated at how—for a single moment—their
burning wings looked like stained glass, parti-
tioned by lead.

Thomas's laughter usually gave him away.
Mother would step out onto the porch with the
slop bucket and send him out to the barn without a lantern—which was punishment enough,
because Thomas was afraid of the dark. I
waited for him at the back door to watch him
run to the house from the barn, and laughed
when he came charging back toward the house,
his legs pumping harder than a mechanical logging mule.

Thinking of my father, I could smell the pine sap that clung to his skin. I wanted to be with him and Mother and Thomas and Grandpa and Grandma. I wanted them there with me, walking the streets, buying storemade candy or watching the city boys pitch pennies on the boardwalk. Yet I knew they wouldn't be happy here. But at least they could be happy for me, if I told them how well I was doing on my own. I decided it was high time to write them a letter. All I could find in the shop to write with was a sheet of the brown paper we wrapped completed garments in and a lead marking pencil, but they were good enough for the task. I sat down at the table and wrote letter after letter until I got it just right.

August 19th, 1869

Dear Mother and Father,

I write with my deepest apologies for any fear or grief I may have caused you in my absence. I love and miss you all. Give my best to Grandma, Grandpa, and Thomas. There are no words to express my regret for hurting you. I can only hope that my accomplishments here in Chicago will please you enough to overlook the foolish act that got me here.

I'm working for a respectable woman named

Aeslynn O'Dell who runs her own seamstress shop. Her family served the king of England as tailors in the years before the Revolution. She came here with her husband when Ireland was struck with a great blight that killed all the crops. Mother, Mrs. O'Dell could stitch circles around us. She makes dresses that would top Mrs. Bowfield's finest any day. She even has one of those sewing machines the minister's wife was always bragging on. She finished a dress shirt in less than an hour just yesterday.

Father, I can't tell you how true your warning has been for me. I never imagined there were so many people on this earth. Something tells me I could go years without seeing the same face a second time.

I love you both and I anxiously wait for your response to this letter.

Love,
Katherine

Sizing Up
a Dream

———❖———

The steam whistle from the textile mill down the street wrenched me from my sleep every morning. I bolted out of bed in a panic, thinking there had been a fatal log jam. The Maustone mill always blew the whistle when there was an accident at the logging camp. My nerves were so ruffled it took a while in the shop to smooth them out. I sat on a wooden bench in a murky room pulling a needle through fabric, making things for people I saw only long enough to collect their addresses for billing and listen to their complaints (which were many) and compliments (which were few).

I'd stand behind the counter, staring at a person I'd never met, watching their lips twist around some rude comment about our sewing or our fees and think back to the general store in Wisconsin. Mrs. Bowfield would listen to complaints with a wide smile. She'd nod and hum a little to show she was listening, but all the while she'd be tugging on the small sign hanging under the extra gas lanterns that said, "Fools who waste their time complaining about matters on Earth will have no words left to describe the beauty of Heaven." I'd remember that sign, smile, then say, "We'll serve you better next time, ma'am."

Elly would shake her head in disapproval, but the Dyer sisters never noticed. They rarely went to the counter. They stayed at their table working in unison like some mythical creature with four hands and two heads. As they worked, the Dyer sisters whispered to each other as if they were in the back pew of a church gossiping about the people who had come to hear the sermon.

When there was no one at the counter, Elly kept her mind on her own work unless she was unhappy with my progress. Then she mumbled to herself for the longest time. One morning, she took up a smock I had basted and said, "Edith, I can't see why Aeslynn let you in the door. You've got eight thumbs for fingers. This is far too tight. Rip it out and do it over."

She dropped the smock in my lap and returned to her end of the table. A few minutes later, I heard her mumbling over her work. She was always clearest when she pulled the thread tight after making a stitch. "Takes her right off the street." Stitch. "Doesn't know her from Eve." Stitch. "Can't sew a lick." This went on until she got tired of hearing her own voice. I wanted to stand right up and say, "And how did you learn to sew? Didn't you ever baste a stitch too tight in your life?"

By the time the church clock struck noon, I was worn to the nub. I wanted to close up inside myself and forget everything. I was tired of trying to get things right, sorry I'd ever left Wisconsin, and almost certain I'd never make my own way. I'd sew myself into a stupor of self-pity, then look at what I'd done. My stitches would be crooked, the thread bunched. "Blast it, Katherine," I'd say ripping the stitches out. "Get it right."

As days passed into weeks and my stitches stretched out long and straight, the Dyer sisters' whispers were almost comforting in their quietness, and Elly started to leave me alone. I even learned to sew a thing or two. In a month's time, I could caste a thousand stitches, each one straight and uniform like a grain of rice. I was beginning to think I could learn any task I set my mind to.

After the shop closed for the day, I had to clean up before I went to my room. I also had to let a young girl named Gillian into the shop. Each night, she worked her way through the shop to collect the scraps left behind after a day of sewing, tied them into tight cubes with twine, then bought them from Aeslynn at two cents a bundle. With the scraps, and some cotton backing sold at thirty cents a yard, Gillian's mother, Sharon, sewed quilts in their home. She sold them to hospitals, hotels, and individuals who heard about her.

For days we whispered our hellos, then set to work in silence in the flickering light of the hurricane lamps set out on the table. Then one evening, I noticed a book poking out of the pocket in her apron and decided to ask her, "What book is that you have there?"

Gillian turned, her pale face blushing, "It's a primer."

"Oh." I nodded, remembering the books my mother gave to Thomas and me for Christmas. Since there was no school in town, she had used them to teach us how to read. She bought them through a mail-order catalog. For me they were wonderful. Thomas, on the other hand, wasn't as happy. The primers disappeared after Mother resorted to putting Thomas into the corner to do his daily reading. I found them years later under the floorboards of the attic.

That short conversation was the start of our friendship. Each night we talked as we worked, recounting the events of our days. Gillian was in the sixth grade, and her class had a room all to itself. I was fascinated by the idea of a building with separate rooms and school desks, and classes in sums, history, and geography. I remembered reading about a new school opening in Chicago, once. I had wanted to attend school so badly. To sit with other girls my age. We could share stories, go berry picking after school, hold tea parties—real ones with cups and saucers and little bowls for cream and sugar. At school, I could read from book after book. Gillian's school had its own library, and she could take any one of the books home with her for a week at a time. Gillian allowed me to borrow books, so thanks to her I learned about things such as the childhood of Abraham Lincoln, the Pilgrims, and the rivers of Illinois.

Gillian once told me, "You know Edith, if it weren't for you, I'd forget half this stuff."

"I love to listen to all your stories," I told her.

"It's almost as good as listening to Grandpa Jacob."

"I wish my grandfather were alive. He was from Germany. Mother says he always talked about his village where goats roamed the streets and there was a clock with a life-sized bear carved out of wood that rung the bell on every hour."

"My grandfather tells great stories, too." I nodded, remembering how Thomas and I used to sit on either side of Grandpa's chair to hear him tell stories. Grandpa spun tales of the past as I picked out the pine needles stuck in his pant legs. He'd settle into his chair and clear his throat, then he'd lean his head back and start by speaking to the ceiling. His wobbly voice echoed through the room.

Gillian sat down on the Dyer sisters' bench and said, "Tell me one, Edith. You're always hearing my stories. I want to hear one of yours."

"All right." I took a deep breath and told the story the best I could, but as I spoke, I heard Grandpa's voice in my head. "The corn on the Lunden homestead was knee high when it was devoured by locusts in 1841. The crop turned to dust and the house was taken away by the bank. With nowhere to turn, Grandpa packed up his family and moved to Maustone, looking for work. After settling Grandma and their boys in a hotel room, he went to the general store, hoping to catch word of a job from one of the many farmers who gathered around the pot-bellied stove for warmth and gossip. They welcomed him with silent nods as he walked up to the stove. He stretched his hands out over the open flames and admired the scars of his hard work.

"His thoughts drifted as he half-listened to the quiet murmuring of the men around him until he heard a booming voice echo out of the corner. 'Mark my words, gentlemen, the great iron horse will carry this country into new lands greater than anything we have ever seen.'"

Gillian laughed to hear me imitate the railroad man. I smiled and kept going. "Grandpa pushed his way through the tight knot of men forming in the corner. Peering over shoulders, he caught sight of a railroad man describing the great iron rails that would bore into the western frontier. Grandpa ignored what he called the romantic lines about open prairies and stout black mountains. He wanted to know what he would get paid if he agreed to leave his wife behind and live out of a tent for several months of hard work. He needed money to put good shoes on his feet, a roof over his family's head, and food in the cupboard. The railroad man offered seventy-five cents a day to any man reporting to the Northern Pacific office in Chicago by the first of February that year."

"Did your grandfather go?" Gillian asked as she leaned forward.

I said, "Before the twenty-second of January, Grandpa and his three sons stood at the office doors with newspapers stuffed in their coats to cut the bite off the cold."

"What did your grandmother do?"

"Grandma stayed in Maustone with her sister and waited for her family to return. Grandpa and my father and his brothers laid the iron and wood that would one day lead the iron horse right to our own Maustone, Wisconsin, not more than an hour's ride from my family's front door. They agreed to stay on and build the line from Chicago to Saint Paul when they were promised an additional five cents a day. They sent their pay home, and Grandma kept it safe behind the bricks in the fireplace.

"By the time the rail reached the eastern edge of Wisconsin, they were laying two miles of track each week. Grandpa said there were days when he thought the company was trying to get them to build the rails fast enough to beat the wagon trains to California.

"They were building a bridge over the Mississippi River when Grandma sent a letter to say she'd run out of room behind the bricks in the fireplace and had put the money in the bank."

Gillian giggled. "My grandma would do that, too."

Smiling, I told her, "Grandpa Jacob and his boys rushed back home on the very same rail they had built. He was back in Wisconsin for less than an hour when he walked out of the bank with a pocketful of money and marched up to Jamison Stokes, who was socializing in Bowfield's general store. He paid Mr. Stokes twice its worth to get the Lunden homestead back into the family. Within a year, my family had built our plank house among the towering pine trees."

"I bet it's beautiful."

I could smell the pine trees. I would have cried if I was alone, but I jumped up and started sweeping instead. I could blame it on the dust if I started.

"That was a great story, Edith."

"Thanks," I whispered. I found myself wishing it was a little more than just a story. I was feeling awfully homesick, and glad to have Gillian there.

Gillian was a fine girl. I enjoyed our time together. Unfortunately, I spent much more time with the women in the shop. We worked from six until dusk in the choking summer heat.

It was almost like the city was so full of tall
buildings, shuffling crowds, and rambling bug-
gies, carts, and wagons that the heat, having
nowhere else to go, packed itself into our shop.
But with all the work, there was no time to
think about the heat, let alone the museums or
libraries I longed to explore. Every morning, I
got up at dawn. I couldn't help thinking of
Mother as I slid out of bed, the room still filled
with predawn shadows. She always woke before
anyone else to start a fire and warm the house. I
imagined her walking down the stairs at home as
I made my way down into the shop. I could almost
smell the pine-scented oil she rubbed on her hands
each morning to keep the skin from cracking.

I had to get things ready for Elly and the
Dyer sisters. They always came in first. Walking from home, they arrived just after six each
morning. Opal would open the door for Louise
and they'd be deep in conversation about something—such as a tale about a woman in the
church whose breath stank of laudanum, or the
outrageous price of fruit at the market.

"Good morning, Miss Shay," Louise would
say, helping Opal take off her coat.

"Morning." I never knew what else to say. I
couldn't figure out if there was such a word as a
plural for Mrs.

Opal would always nod as she passed me to get to their bench, saying, "Edith."

I felt so alone as I watched them each day. Opal would say one word and Louise could finish the sentence. Opal retrieved things Louise needed without being asked.

Elly would usually rush in shortly after them, chattering away about something, a child who cut in front of her to cross the street or a wagon that nearly ran her over. Elly was forever complaining about the rush and the rumble of the city.

One morning, Louise said, "If it bothers you so, Eloise, you should move back home."

"If I had the finances, I certainly would, Louise. Not that it's any of your concern," Elly snapped as she knotted her thread.

"Oh, Elly," Opal teased. "Don't be sore with Sister. She only sees how unhappy you are here."

Elly mumbled to herself.

Louise raised her voice to say, "Speaking of home, did I hear you're from Virginia, Miss Shay?"

I looked up. Louise stared at me with a blank face. The smile on Opal's face reminded me of Reverend Farley after church services. He'd said God bless you to a hundred people and the smile on his face looked painful, as if he had a sneeze that was just tickling to get out.

It was an open invitation to talk about myself, but I was ashamed. Here was a woman who wore a dress that would take up all my clothes in fabric alone. Elly had told me Louise lived in an apartment with her husband, who had a desk job at a shipping company. Opal lived just below them, behind the letter writing service her husband owned and operated. They would have no interest in a girl from a tiny town in Wisconsin.

Now a woman from Richmond, Virginia, who had survived the traumas of war firsthand would have a story to tell. I started searching through my memories of the articles I had read about the siege of Richmond, but I took too long. "Well, are you or aren't you?" Opal asked.

I was speechless. I wanted to tell her I'd carried my two youngest cousins to the caves outside of Richmond, a babe in each arm, as buildings crumbled around me. I could feel the ground shaking under my feet, hear the bombs erupting in air, but I couldn't form the lies in my mouth. Elly was shaking her head in her usual disgusted fashion. I tried to speak, "I . . . I . . ."

"Is she all right?" Louise asked her sister.

"She's just fine." Aeslynn stepped up to the table. "She's just not a talker like you ladies." The Dyer sisters blushed as their shoulders touched. They giggled. Aeslynn tapped me. "Follow me, lass, I want to show you how to make a preacher's collar."

"Yes, ma'am." I bowed my head and scooted off the bench to go to the other room. I was so embarrassed I could have gone all the way out the back door, but I stopped at the sewing machine, then turned around.

Aeslynn came in and pulled the curtain between the two rooms. She motioned to the bench below the window. "Have a seat, there."

I sat down and put my hands in my lap. When Aeslynn put the fabric she held down on her table, I knew we weren't there to talk about sewing.

"Edith." Aeslynn sat down in front of me. "I know I've got no right to pry, but what's the real reason a young girl like you is here in this beast of a city?"

I stared at her. She had her head slightly turned, so she was looking at me from an angle. I thought for just a second that it would be pretty easy to lie if she didn't look me straight in the eye. I silently recited all the reasons I'd given myself: it's a land of opportunity, I could find a husband, see all the museums, read all the books in the libraries, buy fresh apples for a penny a piece in the open market. But we had our own apples not a hundred feet from our front door back home. I hadn't even seen a museum since I'd arrived. I stayed in Chicago because I was ashamed to go home, but I couldn't tell Aeslynn. She'd pity me. I could see it in the sad look on her face.

"All right, if you won't tell me, then I'll tell you a story. Maybe that'll loosen up your tongue a bit."

A story? Aeslynn could pull me in with a good yarn. She never looked at me when she spoke of Ireland; she always stared off, as if she could see the events in her mind and she didn't want anything to interrupt.

"When I was a girl, there was a man Da knew who worked in the textile mill where we bought our cloth. His name was Lyle, Lyle Dorthey. He had ten children. We were beginning to think he'd have to send some kids out into the street to sleep. Every Saturday, Da came home from the pub with another story from Lyle. He was a master at it. Someone in the pub would be moaning about a problem and out of his own hat, Lyle would pull out a long tale. If the fella was listening close enough, he'd realize that Lyle was using a story about someone else to give an example of what could be done about the problem at hand. Only thing was, Lyle always ended his stories without saying what was right or wrong. He left that up to the fella himself.

"Old Lyle considered himself a lucky man. He had a fine, large family, a gift with the tales, a good wife, and steady work. Luck aside, he wanted to give his family something more, so one winter he took up a job telling stories for parties at the manor house. That's the house belonging to the people he worked for. The British snob of a lady he worked for told all her guests they owed it to Ireland to hear the stories of our peasant past. It makes me want to spit when I think on her believing we were nothing more than an isle of beggars, but old Lyle, he jumped at the chance to spin his yarns in some fancy parlor with a grand piano. He spent almost half a year's wages on a suit. He turned a good shilling for near to a month, then he came down with a fever and before the spring thaw, he and half his whole family were dead." Aeslynn finished her story and stood up.

I put myself in Lyle's place. I was as big a fake as he was and Aeslynn knew it, but what did she expect me to do? Did she want me to run back to my parents in shame? I didn't know what to do, so I asked, "Why'd you tell me that story?"

Aeslynn stepped out of the room, then came

back with a velvet hat pinned snugly to her head. "Well now, if I told you what the story meant, then that'd show I didn't learn a thing from Lyle's example, now wouldn't it?"

I took a deep breath and told myself I wasn't a fake. I was still myself, and in time I'd be the seamstress I was trying to be. "I'll get better at the sewing, Mrs. O'Dell."

"I don't give a flying fairy about the sewing right now, Edith. I'm asking about you. Why are you here?"

"I'm working."

Aeslynn suppressed a laugh, "Really now? So where would you be doing that?"

I laughed, wishing my mother could tell a joke sometimes. I started searching my mind, hoping to find a reason that would give me the right to be in Chicago. "I'm working to improve myself."

"Improve yourself?" She smiled. "A fine goal. Fine indeed. What kind of improvements were you thinking of making?"

I could feel the heat rising in my face. I felt like a foolish child talking to such a fine woman about such things. "I want to save up enough for a place of my own and some better clothes."

Aeslynn nodded. "And will you be living your whole life in this place of your own?"

"No, I would like to find a husband." It was

more of an excuse than a reason. The truth was, I just wanted to prove I could stand on my own—show my family I could make a space of my own in the world. Then I could think of courting, finding the man who could take me to see the world.

"Find a husband. Most girls are looking for a husband to find them."

"Oh."

"No, that's fine, Edith. Good, in fact. You seem to be the kind of girl who has her own way of doing things."

"Yes, ma'am."

"A husband, eh?" She nodded looking out the window. "So, what brings you to a city like this? Why not look in the place you're from?"

"The boys where I'm from aren't the type of man I want to marry."

"I see. What type of man do you want to marry?"

I'd thought of getting married. I knew I'd have to someday, and when I did, I wanted a man who would respect me. He wouldn't call me Ma or hit me on the backside while I was cooking. We'd walk side by side down the boardwalk and talk about the way clouds created rain, or plan a trip to Ireland. I smiled, maybe even blushed, as I said, "A man like Mr. O'Dell."

Aeslynn crossed her hands over her chest shouting, "My Ethane? So tell me, what kind of man is he?"

I shrugged saying, "You know he's intelligent and polite."

"Of course." She nodded. "Go on."

"He tips his hat to women in the street. He's traveled all over the world."

"Not all over lass, there's a whole other world out there beyond Ireland and America."

"Well, I've never been to Ireland. You and Mr. O'Dell crossed the Atlantic, then came all the way to Chicago from the East Coast."

"Compared to the trip from Ireland, that bit was a run around a pond."

"I suppose, but I've never been more than thirty miles away from my own house before now."

"Well, Edith, you seem to be a girl who knows what she wants, but you aren't going to attract a man wearing the likes of that." I was wearing one of the three dresses I had brought with me. It was the syrup brown dress my grandmother had sewn with a split collar trimmed in lace, a wood-flower pattern. The hem swung above the top of my boots. "I'm sorry lass, but here, if you aren't wearing a dress fit for royalty, you aren't fit for courting."

Aeslynn grabbed a handful of the fabric of

her dress, then added, "If I wore this dress in front of me ma, she'd think I'd gone to making myself up as the queen herself. Here, dresses like this are as common as blades of grass. There are different dresses fitting for different places, so I'd say you need yourself a Chicago dress. Let's go and see that you're made up proper." Aeslynn held out a hand to lead me out of the shop.

"Now?"

"I can't think of any better time than the moment."

"But the shop . . ."

"It's my shop, lass. I can decide when I want to leave it and who I want to leave it with, thank you very much."

"Of course." I nodded, and we went out the back door onto Kilpatrick Avenue.

"The streets here are a mite strange." Aeslynn looked around at the buildings lining the streets. "You've got enough room from one side to the other to build an entire row of houses or shops. Everything here is so spread out you'd think you Yanks thought you had the world to yourselves."

"In comparison to where I come from, things are crowded here," I whispered.

Aeslynn didn't hear me, so she turned back to the topic of courting. "Men choose their women by appearance. If you're looking dashing, they'll ask for your company. The fact your father isn't here means they'll come to me."

"Come to you?"

"Yes, no man's going to walk up to a strange girl and ask to court her. That wouldn't be proper. Besides, you wouldn't want strange men sauntering up to you now, would you?"

"I suppose not."

"You're not from a city, are you, lass?"

"No, ma'am."

"That explains enough to get me back Dublin."

"Excuse me?"

"That just means I understand a lot more of you now."

"Oh."

"Like I said before, appearances are everything when it comes to attracting a suitor. What you do and say is what keeps him interested, but you have to be attractive to bring him to you in the first place."

As we walked down the street, I couldn't help but think of my mother and all of her attempts to marry me off. In the months before I left, she was always looking for a husband for me. I was sixteen and pretty close to marrying age. Mother was only fifteen when she married Father. Marriage was an unquestionable part of a woman's life. How else was I going to have a house, food, and clothes? Besides, the only women who weren't married were crazy or crippled or widowed. There was nothing worse than being an old maid. I knew I had to get married, but I didn't want the boys Mother chose for me.

Her head would turn when a young man entered church. Her gaze would follow him all the way to his seat, then she'd turn to me as if to ask, "Did you see him, Katherine?" Usually, I had and he was the same callused, dirty boy he had been a week before, except for the fresh shirt his mother had pressed for him.

Mother would make the question official over lunch. She'd push her face into a cheeky smile and ask, "Did you see Brian Matthews in church today? What a fine young man. When I was in the general store last week, Mrs. Bowfield said he looks to inherit his father's farm. Can you imagine that? One hundred and fifty acres of nothing but crops."

"And only a pond's width away from our place," Grandma Margaret added.

I didn't want to imagine spending my life with Brian Matthews, staring across the same pond I'd seen every morning when I woke and pulled up the shade. No boy from Maustone was going to take me away to new, unknown lands.

While my mother was trying to interest me in every local boy my age, I imagined all the far-off places I'd go on the arm of my husband. He would be a lawyer, or a judge called away to bring justice to lawless lands. I'd be there with him, protected by his strength and the respect he commanded. When the Wisconsin wind made my dress feel thinner than it was, I thought of the petticoats and shiny skirts I would wear and the little shops where he'd buy me hats with feathers and bows tied on by careful hands.

I felt I was taking the first step toward finding such a man, that afternoon in late September. Aeslynn opened the door that day to another, private Chicago. We traveled to a small dress shop tucked into the garment district that didn't even bother to display its name on the front window, because the proprietors wanted to keep unsuitable customers from walking in off the street. Their advertising was done by word of mouth. They had dresses that had been hand sewn by the best seamstresses in Chicago, Aeslynn among them. The proprietors, the Mertell sisters, didn't sew, their talent was more unusual. They showed women how to wear the clothing other people made—the perfect dress for a picnic along the lake, the best parasol, the finest shoes, not to mention just the right hat, gloves, and jewelry. Their store was like a library of women's clothing and accessories.

Aeslynn knew the Mertells by their first names, Rachel and Charlotte. They had rings for each of their fingers, wore pearl hairpins, and were ensconced in silk and taffeta dresses that carried on for several feet behind them. Their faces were carefully painted to hide their emotions. The white powder filled the creases in their cheeks that would have shown the effort they put into smiling. To me, the sticky pitch on their eyelashes made them look dishonest.

Rachel Mertell came around the counter with a fan dangling from her wrist. She avoided looking at me altogether. "Mrs. O'Dell, who have you brought to see us today?"

"This young lass works for me, and she needs to prepare herself for suitors."

Charlotte Mertell, a tall woman who resembled a coatrack embellished with taffeta ruffles and ostrich feathers, swung around behind her sister and took my hand. "Aeslynn, dear, you can't be serious. She's a mere child."

"I'm sixteen, ma'am," I said, pulling my hand away from Charlotte's cold fingers.

Aeslynn glanced over her shoulder. Her eyes approved of my response, but her lips were frowning. "She's a young lady hiding in a little lass's clothing, I'll agree, but she's a lady just the same."

I had no interest in becoming a lady by the Mertells' definition. I could see by the put-out look in their faces that the Mertells weren't just fussing over my age. They didn't like the country look of me—my scuffed boots, braided hair, and thick cotton dress. I wasn't a city girl—not prideful and flouncy like they were. I didn't want to be stiff and proper, with more clothes than compassion, trouncing around the room like someone newly crowned duchess. But I trusted Aeslynn and withstood the sisters' transformation. The full, emerald green dress they chose for me required a corset and a bustle. A corset feels like you've slid into a barrel that isn't round enough for you to pass clean through. It forces your arms away from your body and keeps you scrambling for air. Charlotte put her knee into the small of my back and yanked on the strings to tighten the corset, and I was sure one of my ribs would shoot straight out of my mouth.

"There's a figure here somewhere," Charlotte declared, giving the strings another tug.

"Oh yes," Rachel agreed, putting her hands on my newly formed waist. "She looks quite nice." All cinched in, I looked like a porcelain doll with a cloth torso.

The bustle was another affair. It felt like I had an egg basket hanging off my backside. When they put the dress on over the top, I understood why our horse team always shifted their feet when the harnesses went into place. I felt a hundred pounds heavier in the Mertells' outlandish affair, and it took everything I had just to keep my balance. The sisters danced around me with ease, their belled skirts scraping the walls but never slowing them down. Personally, I didn't have the first idea how I was going to move. As it was, I had the sensation I was slowly sinking to the floor.

"What do you think?" Charlotte stood back after she was finally satisfied with the lay of the ruffles around my egg-basket backside. "She's got kind of a small head. Would a hat be too much?"

"A hat?" I screamed silently. Certainly a hat was ladylike, but if they put anything else on me, I was sure to fall over like a dead tree in a strong wind.

Aeslynn who had been standing silently by the front door shook her head. "Call me provincial, ladies, but I would stay with a good snood."

"Snood?" This was a new word that tickled the inside of my nose.

"Right you are," Rachel agreed, scuffing behind

the counter. "Her hair is quite unremarkable. We should spruce it up a bit."

"It'll definitely have to come out of this ridiculous long braid that looks like a bell pull," Charlotte added.

Unremarkable? I had brown hair down past my waist. My mother used to sit at the end of my bed to brush it. My hair was so thick she'd be brushing for an hour. I loved having her strong hands running slowly down my back as she flattened my hair with the brush. If you held my hair to the light, you could see hidden tints of red. I wasn't about to tell the Mertells that. They'd probably suggest I walk around with a lantern strapped to my neck stopping strange men to have them admire the red in my hair.

As it was, they wanted to scrunch my hair up in some fool thing called a snood, which is really just a fancy net for your hair to keep it from shedding strands all over the dress. It wasn't half bad, to tell the truth. It would keep me from sewing any more hair into the curtains I was making at the shop.

"There." Charlotte stepped back after she pushed me into the proper posture. "You look quite fine, Miss Shay, quite fine."

"What do you think?" Rachel asked Aeslynn.

Aeslynn smiled. "She looks like a lady."

I took a step, and the ensemble surged forward. The similarities between the movement of the getup I was wearing and the way custard wobbles when you drop it onto a cold plate made me laugh.

"She likes it, too," Charlotte announced in response to my laughter. "Now, just keep your steps short for a while, young lady. You don't want to trip on your skirts, and for Heaven's sake pick them up when you go upstairs or you'll be facedown before you can snap a button."

Aeslynn pulled her purse strings tight, and I was seized with a greater problem than mobility. "But I don't have the money for all this. . . ."

The Mertell sisters reacted as if I'd taken the Lord's name in vain. They covered their lips in shame as if the words had escaped from their own mouths.

"You're not paying for it, Edith," Aeslynn corrected. "These fine ladies are two of our best customers. They are doing this as a favor to me."

"Thank you." I nodded to the sisters, then turned to Aeslynn, "Thank you, Mrs. O'Dell."

"You'll thank me enough by learning to sew one of these on your own." Aeslynn escorted me to the door. I couldn't imagine why I would want to do such a thing, but I nodded in agreement, to get outside and take some fresh air into my lungs. Wobbly in my new attire, I took the arm Aeslynn offered for support. "Thank you, ladies," she said, waving as we left the shop.

On the boardwalk, Aeslynn squeezed my hand. "Lass, never speak of money in front of a lady. It isn't polite."

"How do people pay for their goods there?"

"They're billed in the post."

"Oh."

We walked in silence for a moment, then I was struck with a queer thought. It had taken two women to dress me, so how was I going to get out of the outfit alone?

I proved to be more agile than I expected when it came to getting undressed that evening. With little difficulty, I had the eyehooks undone and was beginning to slip the dress off over my head. For a moment, I was certain, I'd never come to the hem of the dress as I fought my way through the folds of fabric, but it finally slid over my head and slumped into a wrinkled pile on the bed. The bustle was easily removed. I just unbuckled it in the front and it dropped to the floor with a clank. The corset was another affair entirely. When I reached back to undo it, I tightened it and nearly suffocated. I pulled it from side to side to loosen it, but to no avail, so I held my breath and tried to untie it again. There was a popping sound when I released the strings. I pulled it over my head, then ran to the window to take in some fresh air. When the cool evening air hit my bosom, I realized I was sticking my head out of the window in the middle of a city while I was only half dressed. There wasn't a single pine tree in sight to hide me from the view of the folks walking along the boardwalk. I slid to the floor and laughed until I cried.

After my first "dressing" experience, I wasn't all that certain formal attire was for me. In fact, I saved the dress for my Sundays off when I went to the conservatory or the library. What I did know was that I could learn a lot from Aeslynn O'Dell. In fact, I was right. With her watchful eye, tight-lipped advice, and gracious hospitality, Aeslynn introduced me to the surging energy of a sewing machine. She'd given me so much, and I'd returned so little. I hadn't even told her my real name.

I could see Edith's suitcase from where I sat on my bed. It was leaning against the wall by the door—almost as if it was waiting to leave. I could feel the guilt of my lie like a weight in the back of my heart, but I didn't have the strength to tell Aeslynn the truth. My thoughts drifted to the real Edith Shay. Taking on her name and possessing her suitcase had brought Edith Shay into my life. I had taken her name as easily as I carried her suitcase, but the fact of the matter was there was a real Edith Shay out there. A woman without her suitcase who had lived through the siege of Richmond.

What kind of woman was she? A young woman like me, traveling to see the world? A refined woman like Aeslynn who'd lost her earthly possessions in the Civil War and was seeking a new home? An elderly woman who remembered the horrifying glory days of the Old South when slavery and the old code of cotillions mixed?

When I was lonely and thoughts of my mother only made the loneliness worse, I thought of Edith. At first, I imagined Edith would be the type of person to show me how to be a woman and serve a man as his wife, not teach me how to cook and try to set me up with any eligible man who crossed our path at Sunday services. I created a woman who traveled with a store-bought hat, a fine wool dress, leather gloves, and carefully wrapped packages. She took shape slowly. I developed her in my daydreams as I sat at the sewing machine with the dull whir of the needle lulling me into a stupor.

"You know, Katherine," she'd say, rocking in a chair next to a large window. "I worked as a young woman, as well."

Her voice was low and smooth, in rhythm with the chair. Her face was shadowed by the fern above her, but I could imagine the cloth on her lap. She was embroidering bright red flowers. "I was a seamstress of a different kind. I ran looms for a textile mill. I wove the type of fabric you sew into dresses."

"Hmmm." I'd hum in interest as she told me of the ear-splitting noise and stifling heat. Once I even caught myself acknowledging her out loud with a quick, "I see."

"You see what?" Elly asked leaning forward.

"I meant," I fumbled, "I meant, I think this seam is good." I showed her my work. She just frowned and shook her head.

Even though I spent my days with all those women, I was really alone. We rarely spoke as we worked, so it was easy to slip into memories of dew-covered pine needles and the bubbling pine sap Father used to fix leaks in the roof. It hurt to think of home. I forced myself to think of Edith instead. When I'd start to think of going home and begging Mother and Father to forgive me, I'd imagine Edith walking down the stone path of an enormous garden filled with snapdragons and tiger lilies, saying, "You're a smart young woman. You know there's more to life than land, a home, and a family."

I could almost smell the flowers, as I imagined sitting on a bench beneath a weeping willow tree. "But I want a family, Edith."

"Of course you do." She'd smile, a red snapdragon between her fingers. "We aren't meant to be alone in this world, or God wouldn't have divided his children into two sexes. No, a woman needs a man in this world, but she must be aware of her choice in the matter."

My mother thought she was giving me a choice by offering every eligible bachelor in Maustone, but I couldn't find a man who would show me the world among them. No one like Mr. O'Dell would be hidden in such a small town. But where would I find him? He certainly wouldn't walk into the Royal Stitchery for a new dress.

Sunday afternoons were the only times I really explored Chicago. I took advantage of the free public admission to the conservatory and wound my way through the enclosed city jungle to find the quietest place possible. It was a stone bench tucked under gangly, green plants. It was so nice to feel as if I were in the country again, listening to the birds sing.

There among the stiff green leaves and the

pungent smell of pollen and moist soil, I pushed away memories of towering Wisconsin pines after a spring rain and kept Edith Shay alive and talking.

"You're right Katherine, there are many different kinds of men in this world. There are those who savor the hard work of the open fields. They're just as loving as other men. They simply express it differently. They speak with silent smiles and the care they give to their land. They work for their families, not themselves. You know that, don't you?"

I'd sit with my knees against my chest, hugging my boots with the ivory buttons, nodding. Edith would lean back in her rocker and laugh. "My grandfather was such a man, God rest his soul. He never let an 'I love you' pass from his lips, but he picked the finest watermelon in the garden to cut open for me when I arrived."

I could almost taste the watermelon as she told the story. It was Grandpa Jacob's story really. He always gave me the first slice of the first ripe watermelon every summer.

"There are other men out there as well, men who would rather read a book than meet a fine young lady. Or those rough cowboys who risk life and limb to live in the wilds of the West. And then there are the gentlemen. That's who you seek. A gentleman with a cowboy's spirit for adventure."

Yes, that's who I was looking for. A man who would know exactly what to do with the extra silverware I'd had to set at the Greymore. He could order wine from their wine list, knowing the difference between a burgundy and a blush. He wouldn't call me "Mother" or answer questions addressed to me. He'd turn to face me, saying, "What do you think, Katherine?" when someone asked his opinion. Best of all, he'd love to travel. We'd ride the train into the Appalachian Mountains, take a steamship down the Mississippi, ride horses in the forests of Tennessee, stand on the beaches of the Carolinas and admire the ocean.

But no man like that existed, and if he did, he wouldn't seek the hand of a country bumpkin like myself. Still, I imagined meeting a fine young gentleman who might share the same dreams. If I was to take the hand of a gentleman, I had to find a way to refine myself. Drawn from my imagination, Edith could know no more than I did, and the more I talked with her, the hungrier I got for the facts about the things I imagined. I spent hours in the wooden, echoing rooms of the Michigan Avenue Library, reading Abigail Waters's society column in back issues of the *Tribune*.

• • •

No matter how enjoyable my imaginary stories became, I still had to face the real Chicago. When I added up my first month's earnings, I realized a seamstress position wasn't enough to live on. At twenty cents a day, I was making a dollar twenty a week for a total of four dollars and eighty cents a month. That was enough for two meals a day from Grace's Kitchen across the street, with something left for a weekly newspaper, but nothing more. I could find a second job, but Aeslynn had warned me against that when she hired me. I decided that the best thing to do was to approach her with my problem. Aeslynn was the last to leave every night, so I waited until we were alone, then approached her with my pay in hand. "Mrs. O'Dell? Do you have time for a question, ma'am?"

"Ma'am, is it? You must want a word or two about your pay if you're using such a proper name."

"Yes, ma'am."

"Out with it, Edith. I'm not going to take it back if you have a complaint about it."

"It's just . . ." I couldn't bring myself to look her in the face. "I have to buy food, and the cheapest meal I've found is a bowl of soup for a nickel, but I get hungry before dinner. I just can't live on four dollars and eighty cents a month."

Aeslynn laughed. I'd never heard her laugh, and it startled me. It wasn't light and bouncy like the laughter of most women I knew. It rattled in her throat like marbles in a flour tin. "You are a peculiar one, Edith. You can't look me in the eye, but you can tell me you need more money."

"I'm sorry. I should—"

Aeslynn jumped to her feet. "You should look me in the eye!"

"Yes, ma'am." I looked up, expecting to see her face pulled into a tight frown.

She was smiling. "I don't have more money to give you, Edith. The other ladies have husbands with jobs. They work here to make the little extra money they need to pay the bills. I pay them what I can, and I've paid you what I can.

"Most women who work aren't supporting themselves, Edith. It's a man's job to support a woman. But just the same, I see your point. How about I bring in breakfast for you?"

"Oh, you don't need to do that."

"You'll take my money, but you won't take my food?" She laughed again, and the sound tickled me a little. "I'll be here bright and early with a good, hot meal. Now off with you so I can get home."

Aeslynn went home. I cleaned the shop, then

went to my room and spent the night alone rereading the paper I'd bought a week ago. After a month in the city of Chicago, I no longer believed it was a land of opportunities. It was one giant maze filled with tests and tricks. Aeslynn was there to help, but I had to find a way out or a way up—something that was a bit more than just surviving.

I caught myself thinking that my mother and father would be able to work out a plan. They had found a way to build a plank house in the land of log cabins. They even saved up enough to buy a new stove and ship it all the way from Pennsylvania. They were probably sitting in front of that very stove right now. Mother repairing the latest tear in Father's shirt. He was always catching it on a branch. Father would have his hands around a coffee cup; he loved the warmth of the tin against his skin. The more I began to wish I was there with them, the madder I got. I had come to Chicago to prove I could make my own way, and after only a short time, I was longing to be back home in the warmth of the old kitchen. No, I wasn't going to have it. I could provide for myself. Take a second job. Sew on the side like Gillian's mother. I would definitely make it. Yes, sir. I fell asleep believing just that.

Respect Your Elders

———◆◆———

The post office on Michigan and Seventh was a converted general store. The painted image of the blue speckled coffee pot seeped out around the edges of the postmaster general's sign. The strong smells of coffee beans and ground pepper lingered in the room. Every afternoon for weeks, I'd meet Mr. Quince, the postmaster, at the front door as he returned from lunch. His gold keychain hung out of his pocket as he came up the boardwalk. I was reminded of Buford stepping off the Chicago train with the long watchchain dangling at his side.

I was so sad when there was no letter for me, I didn't have the strength to go right back to the shop to face Elly and her reprimands. To build my strength, I walked slowly back to the shop. I didn't travel on the main streets. To be truthful, the enormous office buildings with their crouching gargoyles gave me the shivers. Aeslynn told me that those frightful stone creatures were once meant to ward off demons, but they scared me to the point that I took the side streets. I enjoyed looking at the tall buildings with shops below and apartments above. It was hard to think of a building as tall as a tree filled with tiny houses inside—enough to give homes to twenty families or more. In some parts of Wisconsin, there were barely twenty families in one county.

And the shops were so tiny, they couldn't carry much at all. The mercantile I had worked in back home could have fit five of those little Chicago stores in their showroom and carried just as many things as all five put together. There was a shop for shoes, one for hats, called a haberdashery—a word that made me think of fairy tales and tiny furry creatures that lived under trees. They even had a store that sold nothing but cheese and bread. Mrs. Bowfield's mercantile didn't sell either of those—you made your own or bartered for them with your neighbor.

Then there were the tall narrow buildings they called townhouses. Three stories high and one room wide, townhouses were for just one family. I couldn't imagine living in such a cramped place. Our house was three times as wide. Our living room wouldn't even fit in one of those narrow places. But I was awed by the flower boxes that hung from the townhouse windows. I'd never seen an ivy plant that wasn't wrapped around the trunk of a tree, and to see one dangling down from a box below a window was like watching a giant beanstalk grow in the backyard.

Most of the flowers were wilted or missing altogether by this time, because the season was beginning to shift. It was hard for me to tell at first, because I was used to trees that changed color with the coming of fall. Our house sat in a dense pine forest, but around the pond grew many kinds of trees that turned red, orange, and yellow in the cooling weather. In Chicago, it was the wind that carried the changing season. It worked itself up to gale force after fighting the waves of Lake Michigan, then blew its way along the streets. Traveling away from the lake, I always felt like the wind was a warm hand hurrying me along.

I became so attached to my afternoon tour of the neighborhood and so anxious for my letter, that I got into the habit of arriving on the post office steps at one o'clock on the nose. One such afternoon, the door was already open when I got there, and Mr. Quince stood behind the counter sifting through the afternoon mail, his balding head pointing straight at me.

"Afternoon, Mr. Quince."

He looked up without a smile, then tipped his chin as he reached below the counter. "Miss Lunden." He lowered his head and read from an envelope. "Miss Katherine Lunden?"

I was rude enough to snatch the letter right out of his hand as I shouted, "Thank you!" I ran the ten blocks from the post office to my room above the shop. I tore the end off the envelope to get to the letter written by my father's stilted handwriting.

October 5, 1869

Dear Katherine,

I write this letter because your mother refuses. Your decision to spend your money on a ticket to Chicago wasn't a surprise. The fact that you could leave your family is what hurt us.

The trip to Michigan should have shown you what a separation from your family really means. Instead, you were glad to leave us. Your letter talks up some woman named O'Dell who is a stranger to our family and our country. Do you place her above your own mother?

> *Katherine, we raised you to be loyal to your family and work with us to keep our land and our home. Your grandfather and I built this house not for ourselves but for you children, and now you've refused it.*
>
> *If you choose to leave us, then we choose to close our door to you. We care for you Katherine, and we wish you well, but we can no longer open our home to you, because you have refused it.*
>
>

Your father,
Albert Lunden

From the first sentence, a storm brewed up in my heart: *Because your mother refuses?* Why would she refuse to write to me? I started to pace the length of the room. Father made it sound as if I'd abandoned the family. I was short of breath, but unsure if I wanted to cry or scream. How could they tell me they loved me, then tell me never to come home again?

I was ready to break things, shatter the window in front of me into a thousand tiny pieces—a rain of glass that would sprinkle onto the street. I raised my hand to strike, but then I thought of blood. The blood on my father's hands as he fought to fit the stones to build our chimney. I began to cry, seeing Mother wipe blood from her face, remembering how she'd been struck by a falling branch when she went out to push the shutters closed during a storm.

I could see them, but I couldn't touch them. I couldn't tell them I loved them. Scrambling to my feet, I ran downstairs. I had to get to the telegraph office, tell my parents they'd made a mistake. I rushed through the shop, Elly yelling after me, "Where are you going?"

Running out into the street, I ran smack into Aeslynn, knocking her to the ground. Her purse went flying into the street. For an instant, I debated whether to keep going or to help her up. She was obviously shaken, her face pale, her hands fluttering as she reached for her purse.

"I'm so sorry," I blurted, reaching down to help her up.

"Where were you going in such a fury?" Aeslynn asked, wiping herself off.

Her question pulled a cinch around my emotions, I was unable to think.

"Edith?"

"I need to send a message."

"You're not making any sense, Edith. What's wrong?"

I should've gone straight to the train station and bought a ticket home, but I said, "I got a letter from home."

"Is someone ill?" She gripped my elbows and leaned over me. "Do you need train fare?"

I shook my head. She was confusing me. "No one is ill. They're just angry."

Aeslynn stood tall. "Told you you've shamed the family by leaving, did they?"

"How did you know?"

Aeslynn laughed. It was low and angry, almost like a growl. "I know because I lived it. My parents think America is a land of savages, and they aren't talking about the Indians. They're convinced that anyone fool enough to live in such a wild land's got to be half mad, willing to sell their soul to stay alive."

"My parents don't want anyone to leave Wisconsin."

"The blessed homeland?" Aeslynn smiled. "Unthinkable."

A laugh bubbled out of me. I couldn't stop myself.

"Don't listen to them, lass. They're not thinking straight. Anyone who puts their heart into soil is half buried. They're not living life as it's meant to be lived. Out in the open." She raised her hands. "Amongst the people. Seeing the world. When Ethane and I have enough money, we plan to see this country of yours. Take a steamboat down the Mississippi. Who knows, we might keep sailing until we bump into South America."

"Really?"

"Walk with me, lass." She slipped her arm through my elbow and started to make her way down the boardwalk. "Let me guess, now. They said awful things in that letter you've got gripped in your hand."

I looked down. I was still clutching the letter. It was all rumpled and torn. I stopped to smooth it out. Aeslynn put her hand over mine. "Don't let them break your heart," she whispered. "They'll never stop loving you, Edith. And when they realize that they can't hold you down with their threats, they'll be begging you to come home."

"Are you sure?" I felt like crying again.

Aeslynn already was. "Me da wrote me just such a letter. Said I was no longer a Kelly in his eyes. No daughter of his would go off and leave the family." She nodded. "A year later, he and Ma started writing every week, sometimes every day, to beg me to come home. Said they missed me so much their hearts were shrinking."

I couldn't hold back the tears. I longed for my parents too much. I needed to hear them. To see them. To know they loved me.

"Don't let them do it, Edith." Aeslynn shook me. "They've got their hands around your heart and they're squeezing it to make you come running home. All parents want to keep their children close at hand, but you won't be a child forever."

Was that it? Did Mother and Father want me to remain a child? Stay under their control? I shook my head, unable to decide. "Shouldn't I write to them?"

"And say what? Please forgive me?"

"I hurt them."

She nodded. "Aye, that you did. And you'd better apologize for it too, but not until you know what you really want. Then you can explain it clearly and help them understand."

What did I want? The same thing as Aeslynn, I believe. I wanted to see the world. But I couldn't do that sitting on a bench in a seamstress shop. I had to save my money. Still, I couldn't have my family believing I'd betrayed them. "I have to let them know how I feel."

She squeezed me. "And you will, just not at this moment. You've got to let the dust settle. Give yourself some time to think."

I nodded, then turned toward the shop. "Thank you, Mrs. O'Dell."

"You're welcome, but where do you think you're going?"

"Back to work?"

"Not today." She turned me around. "You're

walking. Clearing out your mind." She gave me a gentle push. "Now get out of here, I've got work to do."

"Yes, ma'am." I laughed with relief.

Aeslynn walked away. I watched her skirts swagger in the wind, saw the way she carried herself, like a woman who could see the end of the road she was walking and was happy with what she saw. God did the right thing in sending me to Aeslynn O'Dell.

I took her advice and walked the streets. I even set my sights on finding Powell Park. I thought the journey would take my mind off my family, but every lanky boy with blond hair became Thomas until I could see the features of his face. I saw my mother serving coffee in a restaurant, Grandpa Jacob throwing horseshoes in an alley. I really wanted to go home. It was dusk when I reached Powell Park. My legs ached from all the walking; my mind was still spinning. I dropped onto a park bench and wished I could close my eyes and appear on the front porch. I'd watch for the lanterns to appear on the hill. Maybe Father would be singing as he and Grandpa Jacob came into view, "There was a little girl, and she had a little curl." I hated that song, but father often sang it when he could see me from the hill. To set him straight I'd shout,

"My hair's straight as pine needles!" He'd just sing it again.

I longed to be home so much my soul felt heavy, but I wasn't welcome there. I had to write them, but what would I say? A young man came into the park with the long pole to light the lanterns, and I knew I had to return to my room. On the way to the shop, I tried to write the letter in my head, tell them why it was so important that I left Wisconsin, but nothing came out right.

Aeslynn opened the door for me. "I was beginning to wonder if you'd walked into the lake."

I forced a smile. "No, I was just wandering."

She took my arm and walked me to the stairs. "Are you all right?"

"I will be." I almost believed it, too.

"Good, because the ladies are hopping mad that you took off work today."

"Took off?" I turned to face her, but she was already on her way out.

Shaking my head, I went to my room. It started to rain as I got undressed. As the storm picked up, I remembered how Mother used to come to our room when the weather got bad.

My mother may have been tighter than a two-stall barn at times, but she had a generous heart. When thunderstorms rattled our walls, she would come to the bedroom I shared with

Thomas. She'd pull a chair to the middle of the room and tell stories until the storm passed and we could lie down to sleep without the fear of bad dreams.

I could see her sitting there with the long braid hanging over her left shoulder and tiny rosebuds sewn on the front of her gown. Her face was gray in the halflight, her eyes focused on the window, keeping watch for falling branches. She always wrapped her braided hair around her index finger as she spoke. Her voice was as smooth as the surface of a pond on a windless day.

She often told us about the day her family's barn caught fire when she was a girl. She'd been reading a book in her bedroom when she saw the flames reflected in the window. Screaming out an alarm, she sent the whole family scurrying out to try and douse the fire with bucket after bucket of water from their well.

When she talked about fighting the flames, she'd stop to touch her face and recall the heat on her skin. "It was like having a high fever," she'd say, before telling us how Grandpa Vince rushed into action when he saw the sparks floating near the house. He ordered everyone to run for blankets, wet them down, and lay them out on the roof to keep the house safe. Grandpa Vince was a smart man and a quick thinker, but they couldn't move faster than the fire. The roof of the house caught fire before the blankets were even wet. They could do nothing but watch the building burn. They lost everything.

They moved north and settled with relatives in Hayward, Wisconsin. Grandpa Vince worked the coal mines in Virginia to pay for a new house, but it was never built. He died in the mines, and the coal company charged Grandma Marie seventeen dollars to ship his body back to Wisconsin.

I could see my mother's family standing at the train station, Mother holding Grandma Marie's hand, her brother Edward, towering over them wearing the sweat-stained hat he never took off. Aunt Fran was probably pacing the platform when the train rolled in. She never could stand still. They'd all be waiting there with the families shouting and laughing and hugging their relatives. All Mother's family had to greet was a plain, pine box that reeked of death. No wonder she hated train stations.

I woke up in the middle of the night. The storm had stopped, but the air smelled of rain. Even the paper I took out of my satchel felt a little damp. I brought a lantern downstairs to write my parents a letter.

Dear Mother and Father,

I'm sorry that I hurt you, but I have to say my loyalty to you is unshaken. I love you all with my whole heart. I just cannot stay where you have tried to plant me. I also know my dreams cannot be matched with yours. I dream of far-off places and you dream of home. I guess this means we can't be happy living in the same place or in the same ways. Forgive me for not taking your dreams as my own.

As for Mrs. O'Dell, no one can be my mother but the woman who brought me into this world. I merely meant to reassure you that I was in good hands here in Chicago. I'm doing good work, learning a new trade, and making great new friends. Please try to be happy for me.

I hope you can find it in your hearts to forgive me. Always remember that I love you, one and all.

Katherine

I sealed the envelope with wax, then took it down to the post office in the early morning and had it in the mail before Mr. Quince even had time to put out the open sign. I'd said my piece, so it was time to be on my way.

Onward

I spent the next week in a haze of words—rewriting the letter to my parents over and over in my mind until my sentences began to collapse onto themselves and I no longer knew what I had written in the first place. Then I started cursing myself for not sending a telegram. It would've cost me a penny a word, but then maybe they would've telegraphed back. I wouldn't have to wait for their answer. Oh, but perhaps I was better off not knowing what they had to say. I tormented myself until I started throwing stitches over my fingers and pulling them right into hemlines. When she caught me doing it, Elly'd shout, "Do you have your head in a coal bin? Keep your mind on your work!"

For the first time, I was grateful for Elly's taskmaster ways. She got me focused on my work and I was able to pull my mind away from my family troubles. I was thankful to Elly, but it was Aeslynn who reminded me of my real intentions in going to Chicago. I was there to find the means to see the entire country. To experience everything I'd read about firsthand. One day, I would see the ocean, perhaps from a ship. I would climb a mountain. Explore a cave larger than a city. Touch a window of the White House. Chicago was a fine start, but I had to go farther, see more, which I couldn't do without money or a husband.

The Greymore Hotel was the solution to my problem with money. They had an advertisement in the paper every other week looking for kitchen help. If I took a job there and worked in the evenings after the shop closed, Aeslynn would never know the difference. It was bound to be like a ride through a sawmill, but I needed the money.

Mrs. Hessmueller didn't even recognize me when I approached her about the job. I decided not to refresh her memory, just in case I'd left a bitter taste in her mouth by leaving so quickly the last time. Fortunately, I was not put on the night duty again. This time I was hired as an assistant cook on the evening shift.

In a week's time, I discovered just how many muscles the human body contains. I spent the entire day bent over my sewing. My neck was stretched tighter than a pig-bladder balloon. My shoulders felt like I was wearing a cast-iron shawl, and my legs needed the walk to the hotel to wake up.

It wasn't just my body that came alive in the cool evening air. My mind woke up. One evening as I passed a man carrying a newspaper under his arm, I realized I hadn't read a word in print for a week. Me, the girl who had ink-stained hands for most of her life, hadn't had a paper or a book in hand for close to a month. There was no time for it with my two jobs, so I started reading signs and the broadsides pasted up on buildings: A SHAVE AND A BATH FOR 25¢, FOR ONE NIGHT ONLY AT THE ORIENTAL SALOON— JIMMY "BLACK-EYE" DIGGS WILL FIGHT MARSHAL "CRUSHER" TIBS. COME ONE! COME ALL! BRING YOUR BETTING MONEY! I dreamed of that bath, loosening my tired muscles, and heard the shouting and screaming of men cheering on the fighters. I couldn't stand the sight of blood, but I longed for words that brought another part of the world alive for me.

I felt so closed off and worn out by both my

jobs that any words at all had the power to send me on a flight of fancy, but that wasn't an option in my work at the Greymore. As assistant cook, I was responsible for everything the cook didn't have the time to do, so I stood in the kitchen for hours at a time putting ridges into the frosting on cakes, cutting shapes into pie crusts, whipping cream into froth, and slicing the meat selection for the evening. The work pulled the knots out of my shoulders and moved them into my arms. My feet blistered and my legs filled with rocks. By the time I walked home, I could feel every muscle in my body move. It was the first time in my life I didn't dream.

Eventually my reading daydreams disappeared and I found my mind wandering through time-saving devices for basting stitches, hemming, frosting, and cutting. Working was the only thing I had to think about. I cut out the chatter of my coworkers and kept to myself. I even found myself rushing Gillian along. I often answered questions in a clipped word or two, and ignored her altogether when she talked about school. My goal was to save twenty-five dollars, more than enough for tickets and traveling expenses for quite some time. I was sure I could raise a reasonable sum in a few months.

One Sunday evening, I entered the dining

room with a platter of roast beef. My foot caught on a runner they put down to keep the carpet from wearing out. I fell full-body onto the platter, splattering gravy all over myself, the buffet table, and the cream-colored gown of one of the hotel patrons. The guests gawked at me.

The cook picked me up off the floor and herded me into the kitchen, apologizing profusely to the guests. "Go clean yourself up, Miss Shay. We need someone to cut the cake." The cook leaned into the hallway as I stumbled to the water closet, "Harriet, get in to the dining room. Miss Shay has gracefully deposited the main course on the floor!"

The shards of the platter had cut into my hands and my chest. I was streaked with blood, and it felt like I'd been sprinkled with hot ash. I was shaking so much I could barely keep a towel under the spigot to wet it. Mrs. Hessmueller burst in as I tried to wipe myself off. "You will pay for this, young lady. The guests have lost their appetite. Three of them left the table!" Shaking a finger in my face, she yelled, "And don't come back until those cuts have healed. I won't have the guests seeing them."

I went home to nurse my wounds. I was covered with tiny cuts. They hurt, but the biggest damage was to my savings. Mrs. Hessmueller sent over a bill the next morning. It arrived before the Dyer sisters did. I was charged $8.70 for the price of the meat, the platter, cleaning the cream gown, and the money the hotel lost because of the reduced customer spending.

I was muttering to myself over the loss of money when Louise and Opal arrived. I heard them gasp. Looking up, I saw them frozen like deer when you catch them in a clearing. "What on earth happened to you, child?" Opal rushed to sit at my side.

"I fell with a plate in my hand. It's nothing really." I pulled away when she tried to examine my bandaged hand.

"Heavens." Louise went to their bench, but didn't take her eyes off me. "You need to take care of yourself. Opal and I were just talking about that the other night."

I looked to Opal. She said, "That's right. Sister and I worry about you. If you were to fall and hurt yourself, no one would be here to help you."

"Young women shouldn't live alone," Louise added, inspecting the work she'd done the day before.

"That's right." Opal patted my shoulder as she stood up. "A young woman like yourself should at least have someone around to look after her."

"I can take care of myself."

Louise pointed to my hand. "We can see that, Miss Shay. In fact, I'd say it's painfully clear."

Those women had me tied into knots by the time Elly showed up. Taking her wrap off, she asked, "What's the ruckus?"

"Miss Shay hurt herself."

"It's no surprise with the way she goes running around. Let's get to work."

It was the first time I was glad that Elly didn't tolerate much idle chatter. We all set to work, and I could've forgotten about the whole embarrassing incident if only I didn't have the bill to pay and my fingers weren't so stiff.

Aeslynn saw the cuts that afternoon when I brought her the collars I had finished. "Is everything all right, Edith?" She looked at me out of the corner of her eye as if she didn't want to pry.

"Just fine."

"Good." She smiled. "Just a little accident then?"

"Yes, ma'am."

"Good." She patted my hand. Mother would have cursed me for being so clumsy, then cleaned out all the cuts with soap and water before bandaging them. Not another word would be said about it. I longed for her.

While my cuts healed, I had my evenings to myself again. As I lay on the bed hearing the sounds of the street below, I realized how much space there was between me and the next person in the world. Even if I went out into the street and introduced myself, people wouldn't know me. They certainly wouldn't understand me. Heavens, even my own parents were angry at me for being myself.

I wondered about Edith Shay. The real Edith Shay. She had been traveling. Probably alone. Her beat-up old suitcase said she didn't have much money. I opened the suitcase to take in the sour-sweet musty smell of Edith's dress and finger her packages to guess their contents. I'd done this so much over the weeks, the brown paper had soaked up the oil from my probing fingers and turned dark brown. Each time I examined them, I thought to open them, but it didn't seem right. The proper thing to do would be to return all her things in the best condition.

By holding the dress against me, I could see Edith was a smaller woman—the hem only came to my knees. I searched for any clues that would build an identity out of the contents in the suitcase, but beyond her choice of clothing, her home address, and my guesses at the contents of her packages, she was an empty picture frame in my head. In my loneliness, I constructed a new picture of the type of person I longed for her to be. In my mind now, Edith was all the people I needed to keep me going, to hold me up and push me forward to become something more than myself. She was an excuse to dip inside my own imagination and develop a sense of independence. In a way, Edith became my family.

Without my family, friends became quite important. Gillian was the only friend I had close to my own age, but she saw me as an adult. One evening, I was disassembling the sewing machine to remove the thread wound around the interior spools. My hair kept separating itself from the bun on top of my head, so I had to tuck it back in. I sat up to redo my hair and stretch the muscles in my back, only to see Gillian coiling her hair on top of her head. She didn't see me watching, so I continued to do so. She pulled straight pins out of the cushion on Elly's work table and started thrusting them into her makeshift bun.

"Gillian, you'll be putting holes in your head before you hold any hair in place," I said as I approached her. She was the only one there, so I felt safe enough to be myself.

She dropped her hair, sending pins tinkling across the floor. "Sorry Miss Shay, I wasn't stealing. I was going to put them back."

"Who said anything about stealing?" I pulled a bobby pin out of my hair and held it out. "You need these to keep your hair up."

"I've seen those in the store." Gillian pointed. "My mom has a little wire cage she puts over her hair."

"You aren't far from the mark." I smiled. "This is chicken wire."

"Chicken wire?"

"Yes, it's fencing to keep chickens in the yard."

"They keep chickens behind fences?"

"When you live in the woods, you have to keep them penned up or they get lost in the trees and live off pine nuts. Next thing you know, your neighbors are dining on your chickens."

"My mother says I have to wait until I pass the diploma test before I can wear my hair up like everyone here does. My sister Marie didn't pass the test until she was twenty-one years old and she was pregnant. Her husband had to bring her in all the way from Wheaton so she could take the test. He was hotter than a canning jar fresh out of the pot over the whole thing. Like Papa, he sees no need for women-folk to be reading and writing. They have no time for it once they start a family."

"Mrs. O'Dell reads every day on her lunch break."

"No offense, Miss Shay, but Mrs. O'Dell doesn't have any children."

"Right you are." I nodded. "Say, how about I put your hair up for you when you're through here?"

"That would be fine. I'm not due back home until six, and I have most everything bundled already."

"All right, I'll finish with the sewing machine and we can go up to my room."

Gillian leaned into my room as if it were a dark, forbidding cave. "I've never been in here before. The old man who used to own this place lived up here. Some say he died in his sleep and he haunts the place because he hates Irish people like the O'Dells."

"Nonsense." I walked past her and pulled up the shades to let in the evening sun. "The only things up here are me and the dust."

"You going somewhere, Miss Shay?" Gillian fingered the cracked leather on the suitcase at the end of the bed.

"No, I just don't like keeping it under the bed. It's too dusty." I went to the bureau for my brush and pins.

"E-dith Shay, 19-19 Fill-more Lane, Rich-mond, Vir-gin-i-a." Gillian read the tag on the suitcase aloud. "Miss Shay, are you going home for Christmas?"

The question hit me like a snowball square in the face. I could feel the melting ice and snow run down my back. Christmas was a time of year that filled our house so thick with good smells, singing, laughter, and gifts we had to open the windows a crack to breathe. It was such a natural part of my life, I had never thought about being without it. To keep my mind from dwelling on the subject, I answered as quickly as possible, "No, I don't have the money." That was true enough, but it wasn't the reason I couldn't spend the holidays with my family. My father's letter rang in my ears as I brushed Gillian's hair into a bun.

I write this letter because your mother refuses.

I had sinned against my mother by stepping outside her sacred Wisconsin. She didn't even want to address me in person.

You were glad to leave us.

My family believed that I wanted to leave them behind, but they didn't know how much I missed them. They hadn't watched me follow strangers down the street because of their resemblance to those I love.

The trip to Michigan should have shown you what a separation from your family really means.

Separation from my family meant not sitting at the kitchen table on Christmas Eve with Grandma Lunden sealing the presents for my small cousins with hot wax. The house filled with noises that kept my hands moving for fear we'd get caught. Everyone came to our house for the holiday, and it was filled from floor to outhouse with people. My cousins had to bed down on the floor and they often rolled in their sleep. Grandpa Lunden and his oldest son Earl were sure to have a snoring duel before the rising of the Christmas sun. Mother and her sister Fran traveled around the room filling the stockings hung from the walls. They whispered to each other to keep their sibling secrets.

I wouldn't be there to sew another patch on the Christmas quilt that had been in the Lunden family for seventy-five years. Grandma Lunden had been there for forty-nine of those years as Grandpa's wife and she was bound and determined to see the backing put on before she was placed in the ground to rest. It took twelve months to choose the right patch of fabric.

When Gillian spoke, she startled me into listening. She said, "We go to my Grandma's house in Michigan every year. Father works at a store packing Christmas boxes to be sent in the mail, so he can pay for the trip. I wonder if they got any more jobs like that so you can have one? Father says there are two women who address the packages."

"Really?" I said.

"Yes, ma'am." She nodded, pulling away to have a look at the finished product. "I could ask my father if you like."

"No, but thank you, Gillian."

I fell back into my thoughts of Wisconsin, and didn't hear Gillian leave. I wanted to hear my mother sing "Silent Night." I longed for the off-key squeal in her voice when she tried to hit the high notes, but I knew I couldn't go home for the holidays. I had to make do where I was.

I soon discovered I was doing a little better than making do. In early November, after I started back at the Greymore, I worked every day on a dress. And with the chill of fall that began to sneak into the lake winds, I stayed up after my shift at the hotel to sew a coat. I started with a wool blanket from a neighborhood mercantile and scraps from the shop—a sure way to keep warm and save my money.

Aeslynn was going to sell the dress—to the Mertells if I did a good enough job. Sewing a dress was a long ways from the sheets I'd started out repairing only months earlier. The coat was no mending job either. To tell the truth, I didn't know a coat pattern from a pea-soup recipe. But I had certainly made a dress before. In fact, I'd sewn my first one with Grandma Margaret when I was ten. Still, this dress was more than that. It was a gown. The fabric I chose was deep green, the color of the spread on my parents' bed. I sewed black sequins onto the bodice in large flourishes. The collar and cuffs I lined with a stiff, black lace that had to be fastened without visible seams. The train quickly consumed seven yards of a fine polished cotton. After three failed attempts, I was able to complete the bow that rested on the bustle.

I even learned a thing or two about making a coat from the dress pattern. My collar was lace-less, but a pretty fine copy of the one I made for the gown. And I had a coat with a bustle for the first time in my life. I even used fabric from the dress to line it. It looked like a coat made from a blanket even with the bustle, but it was warm and I didn't have to run around the city with the bed quilt over my shoulders.

When I was finished with the dress, Aeslynn took it from me. She leaned over it, examined each seam as if she were looking for flecks of gold. Turning it inside out, she continued her search until she finally came to the last piece of the bottom hem. Then she dropped it into her lap and sighed. "A masterpiece." She smiled.

"Really?" I felt so good. I was glad Elly wasn't there to add her opinion.

"The Mertells will sell it before the smell of your sweat leaves the fabric."

That was on the seventh of December, and on the seventeenth, Charlotte and Rachel Mertell came waltzing into the shop, all rustling ruffles and powdered smiles, with the announcement that Mrs. Roberta Babcock, wife of Ellison Babcock, one of the most prominent men in the Chicago shipping business, had purchased my dress.

Aeslynn stood beside me. She was so happy she kept squeezing my arm and laughing, saying, "You did it, lass. You did it."

Indeed I did. I suddenly understood why the shop meant so much to Aeslynn. She was so proud, she invited me to her house for dinner that night, and I knew I'd have the chance to see what a life in Chicago could lead to.

Aeslynn held the door open for me. "I'll give the key to Gillian. She's a fine girl. She'll lock up."

Gillian agreed to do just that, then Mr. O'Dell arrived to escort us to their home. He didn't grip my hand like the handle of an ax as Thomas always did. Instead, he stiffened his wrist and pressed my fingers onto his so that I could use his arm to pull myself into the wagon. It was a gesture of respect and independence I rather enjoyed.

"You look quite fine, Miss Shay." He nodded in my direction with a smile as he signaled the horses to go. I blushed.

The O'Dell house, which stood in a street that curved around a small pond, was everything I ever dreamed of in a family home. When I stood on the front lawn, it looked tall enough to rival the pines which surrounded our plank house in Wisconsin. Their house had shingles painted a faint shade of blue, not shaved planks with moldy green spots caused by rain. The front door had an oval window of etched glass. As I entered the front room, I half expected to find Edith Shay resting in a high-backed rocking chair with knitting in her lap.

We had dinner in a room set aside for the long, polished table Aeslynn covered with a white macramé tablecloth. The meal was served on plates rimmed with silver. They captured the light from the gas lamps on the wall in tiny stars of reflection. My water was as clear as the crystal glass that contained it. There were so many things to see I barely found time to eat. Aeslynn noticed my preoccupation and smiled. "Not like your own home?"

"No, ma'am. Everything in our home's rough-hewn. Nothing has a shine like your things do. Except of course, the windows after a good spring cleaning, and my grandfather's watch."

Aeslynn bowed her head for a moment. Before she looked at me again, she exchanged glances with her husband, who motioned with his fork to encourage her to speak. "My parents weren't well to do. I grew up in a house no larger than this one, and half of it was taken up by our shop."

I couldn't keep the shock from filling my face with heat. I brought my napkin to my lips to hide it, but wasn't successful. Aeslynn continued, "Don't act so surprised, Edith. You wait and see. You'll attract a man like my Ethane." She gripped her husband's hand. "He'll buy you all this and more."

Was that why I was looking for a husband? To buy me things? Take me places? I felt small. Surely that wasn't why Aeslynn was with Ethane.

As Aeslynn served the salad, Ethane said, "The world is changing so quickly, you'll have much more than we do."

"Really?" I nodded, seeing Aeslynn pick up the small fork with three tines to eat her salad.

Indeed, she knew what it was for. There was wine chilling in a silver bucket. I thought they called it a tureen or was that for soup? It was hopeless to try and remember all of those things.

I looked into the parlor through the doorway. I could see the hanging plants, the fine furniture. My Edith was no more than a shadow of Aeslynn. I felt so daft for retreating into my own fantasy when there was a real woman right in front of me who could teach me so much.

"What's this for?" I asked, holding up the fork farthest from the plate.

"Dessert," Aeslynn said, smiling.

After dinner, we went into the parlor. I was amazed at all the wood in the room. Wood paneling, wood floors, wood fireplace, wood furniture, I imagined I'd turn to wood if I stayed there too long. We opened an atlas on the floor and selected places we wanted to go. Aeslynn picked the Gold Coast of Africa because she'd heard it was the center of the grandest kingdom of the continent. "That's of course before the high and mightiness of Europe saw fit to destroy everything in their paths."

Ethane pretended to shiver. "Don't get her started on the empires of Europe, she'll turn into Rob Roy before our eyes."

"Rob Roy was a damned Scot!"

"And your great-grandfather wasn't?"

"Aye, tar feathers. Forget I said a word."

It was wonderful to see them argue. It made me think of Grandma Margaret yelling at Grandpa Jacob for voting for Stephen Douglas.

As Mr. O'Dell drove me home, I couldn't help but think Aeslynn would be in Chicago forever. But there was nothing stopping me from leaving, then returning some day. After all, Aeslynn herself said life should be lived in the open amongst the people, seeing the world. I had to leave Chicago, and soon. If I didn't, I'd stay forever. I'd disappear right into Aeslynn's life with the fancy dresses, the gorgeous houses, the dreams of travel that never get lived.

I'd had enough of dreams, so I agreed to work at the Greymore Christmas Eve when Mrs. Hessmueller offered me an extra fifteen cents an hour. Aeslynn and Ethane had invited me to their home, but I lied to them and said I was spending the weekend with a friend I had met at the library and her family.

That night, the sound of carolers rose up from the street as I stirred the plum pudding to be served at the Christmas banquet (attended for a price higher than my weekly salary). I

A. LaFaye

served the meal with a smile on my face for fear
Mrs. Hessmueller would dock my wages, but I
felt hollow. It was almost as if I were a ghost of
myself floating around that table.

I don't remember cleaning the kitchen that
night, but I knew it had to be spotless before
Mrs. Hessmueller would let me leave. I heard
the carolers singing "Joy to the World" as I
stepped outside into the frigid air. The night
was clear, the stars bright, the sky a blue like the
velvet in the case for the Lunden family Bible. I
found the carolers as they crossed into a park
and followed them until they wound past the
shop, then I went in. From my window, I
watched them move slowly down the street.
I thought of home and the tart smell of pine and
snow on our front porch.

I took out my father's letter and read it again.
I had to force myself to believe Aeslynn. They
would ask me to come again, someday. In the
hope that they would do it soon, I wrote them a
letter. Sprawled out on the floor, the paper
before me, the pencil in my hand, I couldn't
help recalling all of the times I had lain like that
in the attic looking at the newspaper.

December 24, 1869

Dear Family,

I cannot let this day pass without telling you just how I feel. I'm alone in my room, imagining all of you gathered around the Christmas tree singing carols. Mother, I can hear you singing "Silent Night." I know Father has polished up his harmonica and Thomas is snapping along with him on a set of Mother's good silver spoons. Grandpa Jacob, I bet you're telling them all about the Christmas you and your brother Quinton got caught in the snowstorm on the way back from Maustone and the young ones thought you were white bears come to eat them. Grandma Margaret, we're a square closer this year! That quilt will be done before your day comes or we'll bury you in it.

If Aunt Fran is there, please ask her to forgive me. I did not mean to abandon her and will repay her the expense of my ticket as soon as I can. I hope that Uncle Charles is well and giving piggyback rides to all the young ones. He's the only one tall enough to get them up to a height where they can hang the mistletoe from the rafters.

God bless you all. I miss you. Please forgive me.

Love,

Katherine

As I wrote the letter, I imagined myself sitting in the parlor with my family. As I put it in the envelope, I thought about what my family would do when they received it. Mrs. Bowfield would walk it over to the mill where Thomas worked. He'd rush home shouting, "A letter from Katherine!"

Mother would grab it and read quietly to herself. Father would take it as the family gathered around the fireplace. He would read it out loud and comment on everything I said with fondness. Grandpa Jacob would hear Quinton's name and lean back in remembrance, saying, "Oh that night! It was so bitter cold." Grandma Margaret would have to squeeze his knee to keep him from telling the entire story.

Mother would snicker at the suggestion that we'd bury Grandma Margaret in the quilt and say, "Not a chance, Mother Lunden, that quilt's going to be on my daughter's wedding bed."

The truth of the matter was, they might not even read the letter, since they no longer considered me a welcome member of the family, but I felt a strong connection to them just from writing it. I knew I could never stop sending them letters, so I had to pray they would read them and find something within my words that would let me back home.

I felt so alone, so afraid that I'd never see

them again. I prayed to God that he would carry me back to Wisconsin that very night. Dropping onto the bed, I started to cry, then I realized it had been my choice to go to Chicago. I'd decided to stay even after my parents sent me that letter. I'd declined the invitation from Aeslynn and Ethane, so I had to make my own Christmas.

I emptied the suitcase onto my bed. I picked up my favorite package. I'd decided that I deserved a present for keeping the suitcase so long on Edith's behalf. I knew just the one I wanted. I knew it had a book inside—the outline of the grooves in the binding was permanently pressed into the paper because I'd fondled it so much.

Whoever she was, Edith Shay loved someone enough to buy them a book, a thick, paper slice of another world. That someone was without the present I held in my hand. I silently promised him or her that I'd replace the book before I returned the suitcase. It was a leather-bound volume of a novel called *English Orphan* by Louise White. The leather was a deep red, like wine I'd served at dinner. There was a picture of the main character, Daphne, in a straw bonnet with a blue ribbon hand-pasted on the front cover.

I started to read. Daphne was an orphan from England who had come to America to seek out an aunt who'd left England when Daphne was still a small child. Reading was usually my key to another world, but with each new page I found myself walking along the sleigh-rutted road to our house. I could see the wreath on the door, hear my family singing inside. I could even see myself opening the door, everyone turning to see who it was, but would they be happy? I fell asleep praying that they would.

I dreamed of a house, but it wasn't my family's. When I crested the hill that overlooked our house, it wasn't there. I was staring down into a rich, green valley. All I could see were fields lined with wooden fences. Then I turned and saw a grand old house with full-length porches, set back from the road. Black shutters accented the multipaned windows. The road leading up to the house was lined by maple trees leaning over the gravel. Somehow, I knew the house I stared at belonged to the Shay family of Richmond, Virginia.

Children played in the front yard—their laughter bouncing off the walls of the house and drifting out toward the road. Lanterns lit several windows opened to the sweet Virginia air. In my dream, I approached on bare feet, but the gravel didn't hurt. The flagstone of the front porch was as cool as river ice without the bite.

The smoke rippling out of the twin chimneys was black, the exhaust of a good coal fire. My dream ended just as someone, probably Edith, was opening the door. I only saw the outer edge of a pale gray wool dress.

Waking up alone with Father's letter open on the bedside table convinced me I couldn't go home. I suddenly knew that waiting for their letter in Chicago meant I was letting them hold me down. Aeslynn told me I shouldn't let them do it. She said life was meant to be lived out in the open. What was open about a stuffy, dark seamstress shop? Yes indeed, I would see the world.

I jumped off the bed, my feet hitting the floor with a thud because I hadn't even taken off my boots. Laughing at myself, I shouted, "I'll be off!"

But to where, I thought. Minneapolis? Nebraska? How long would my money last if all I did was travel? I started to pace, knowing I was fast on my way to convincing myself that traveling was a foolish dream. Then I saw Edith's suitcase open at the end of my bed. Edith had traveled halfway across the country with nothing more than a change of clothes and some gifts. She'd done it; I could do it. Heavens, she could tell me all about traveling. I could learn all the secrets of touring the world from her. The least I could do was give her back her suitcase. At that moment, I felt guilty for not arranging to return her things earlier. I worked myself up to the point that I thought it was my duty to place that suitcase in her hands face to face. To do that, I had to go to Richmond, Virginia.

I was a fool to think I could just waltz onto a train and ride comfortably down to Virginia to hand over a wrinkled old suitcase to some stranger. But I thought I was doing the right thing. I was putting Edith before myself and returning belongings that were rightfully hers. I'd coveted them far too long as it was.

I kept the most important facts tucked deeply into the folds in the back of my head. It would have been simple to send her a letter and tell her I had her suitcase. With a little more effort, I could have sent the suitcase in the mail, but I needed something physical, something real that could pull me forward to explore the world I'd read about in the papers. I was foolish enough to think that somewhere I'd find the places I'd read about just as I'd imagined they would be.

The first thing I did on the twenty-sixth was go straight to the Fifth Street Station. The ticket clerk at the first window was pulling loose threads out of his vest. "I know of a good seamstress who could fix that for you," I offered.

"My wife's a darn good seamstress, thank you very much," he insisted, the wrinkles around his purplish lips increasing as he closed his mouth. I didn't know how to respond, so I was silent. "Do you want something, or were you just trying to advertise for some tailor shop?"

"I want to know how much it would cost for a ticket to Richmond, Virginia."

"You can't get there from here. Besides what do you want to go to Rebel country for?"

"There are no trains going to Richmond?"

"Sure, southern trains. They didn't want Union-made track so they laid their own and just like their army, their rail isn't built right. It's as thick as their heads. No Union trains can go down there."

"Can I take a southern train?"

"If you can get to a big city close by the Mason-Dixon Line, like Washington, but our line only goes as far as Philadelphia. You'll have to switch over to a different rail company down there. The ticket to Philadelphia's six dollars one way. Train leaves every day at four P.M. and reaches Philadelphia three days later at six A.M. Chicago time."

"Thank you, sir." I wanted to buy a ticket, but then I thought of Aeslynn. I owed it to her to tell her before I did.

"Changed your mind, did you? Smart girl," he shouted after me.

I spent the night trying to find a groove in my mattress deep enough to disappear into. Faces kept sneaking into my head and repeating themselves over and over. There was the woody old man from the Michigan train station who was sure I needed a handout, the powder-faced Mertell sisters who could only see me as a child with unremarkable hair, and the prune-lipped ticket clerk who kept rattling off the reasons why I couldn't go to Richmond. By morning, I was convinced I had to go to Virginia just to prove it could be done. Returning Edith's belongings and meeting her face to face would make it all worthwhile.

My biggest obstacle was telling Aeslynn I was leaving. I felt as if I was betraying her by going. She had been so kind to me, giving me a job, a place to stay, the prettiest dress I'd ever owned. Each night as my coworkers left one by one with half-hearted farewells because they knew they would return in the morning, I tried to get up the courage to tell Aeslynn, but I never uttered a word except good-bye as Ethane tapped at the door to take her home.

Accustomed to living in a house filled with people, I always felt as if I shrank inside when the others left, especially the Dyer sisters. I never really developed a strong relationship with them. It just hurt, in a melancholy sort of way, to see the bond between them, the way they'd stand at the door straightening each other's clothing, buttoning each other's coats, doing everything to make sure that the other was ready to face the winter cold. They walked shoulder to shoulder down the boardwalk and tipped their heads in unison to the people passing by. I wanted someone to look after me that way.

After everyone had gone, the shop would slowly fill with a sense of loneliness. Any movement would make me think someone was returning because they had forgotten something. When I convinced myself no one was coming back, I started to see people in the things around me. The Dyer sisters were creating matching dresses for the Mertells to wear at the New Year's Ball sponsored by Potter Palmer to christen his new hotel on State and Monroe. The sewing forms cast shadowy figures across the floor, making it appear as though the sisters were walking hand in hand across the sewing room.

One night, Aeslynn stayed late to finish the edges on the buttonholes of a pink dress with pearl white appliqué on the bodice. With the thread wrapped around her finger to keep it taut, she kept her eyes fixed on her work. It seemed like just the right time to tell her I was leaving. She was so involved in her work, she might not even think about my words until I was safely inside my room where I couldn't see the pain in her eyes.

"Mrs. O'Dell," I said as I stared at the shoes she'd given me.

"It's Mrs., is it?" She didn't look up.

"Yes." It felt as if someone had sat on my chest, but I kept talking, for fear I'd never have the courage again, "I have to put in my notice, ma'am."

"Do you now?" She made it sound as if we were discussing the right stitch to use when finishing off a preacher's collar on a wool coat.

"Yes, ma'am."

"When will you be leaving?"

"The end of this month, ma'am, but I'll be sure to finish that curtain order for the Grace Brothers Hotel."

"That's good." She turned the fabric over in her hand to examine her work.

"Then . . . then . . . ?" I didn't even know what I was trying to ask her.

She finally looked up. Her eyes were glassy with tears. "You think I haven't seen the way you skulk around here each day. Or the dark circles under your eyes? You've been working two jobs to save up, haven't you?"

"Yes." I was crying too.

"As you should, Edith. You've got a good wild heart in you. And wild hearts should roam." She took a deep breath. "I just wish I could go roaming with you."

We both smiled. "Thank you." I squeezed her hand.

"Ahhh." She shook my hand away. "Off with you. Get to wherever you go at night. You're making me cry!"

I kissed her on top of the head and ran out the door. As I made my way down a side street, it felt as if I could run for miles. I was really going. Really leaving. Amen.

Trust

———◆———

Aeslynn and Ethane offered to buy my ticket and drive me to the station as a farewell gift. I accepted because I knew they wouldn't accept no for an answer. I sat between them, Edith's suitcase between my knees. Ethane was humming a tune I didn't know. He kept his eyes on the road. Aeslynn kept putting her gloves on, then taking them off.

"First my hands are cold, then they're hot," she shouted over the clatter of the street.

I didn't know what to say. Anything about her gloves seemed foolish. Besides, I had a feeling Aeslynn didn't care a fig about them either. "I sure do appreciate your kindness, Aeslynn. And not just the ticket. You've been so generous to me from the start. The job, the room, the sewing lessons . . ." I blathered through a list of things I was thankful for and even tucked in a few things I wanted my family to hear. Aeslynn listened in silence, as a smile spread across Ethane's face.

When we got to the station, Aeslynn went in to buy my ticket. Ethane squeezed my elbow. "Lass, I think it's only fair to tell you my wife hasn't stopped talking about you since the moment you arrived. She thinks you were God's answer to her prayers for a daughter, so don't you go on about how much she's done for you. As far as she was concerned, it was her job."

I barely felt Aeslynn's hug on the platform. Ethane escorted me to the stairwell. I wanted to cry. It was like leaving my mother all over again, but it hurt more. On this trip, I'd miss both her and Aeslynn.

Aeslynn had purchased a first-class ticket, and I held it in my gloved hand. I rushed to my seat to wave good-bye, and the ticket was folded in half by the time I had my face against the window. I stared intently as I waved. I wanted to take in all the details of Aeslynn O'Dell's face. I wanted to be able to recall everything about her, from her resounding Irish voice right down to the way the curl of hair always fell over her left eye as she worked.

Once the train got underway, I pushed myself back into the seat. A first-class ticket meant soft velvet seats, not bristly mohair working its way through clothing to prickle my back. I took in each detail of the train as if it were water after a long trip on a dusty road. The polished wood walls felt like glass under my fingertips. I rubbed away each print I made, to leave the wall just as I had found it. Someone had taken the time to iron out the white linens placed over the back of the seats. They were stiff to the touch, but without so much as a piece of lint. The blue, rippled swags over each window swayed to the rhythm of the train like the current of the Wabash River on a sunny day.

I thought of the old plow bridge over the river. We called it the plow bridge because my great-grandfather Warren had built it so he could take his plow from one side of the river to the other. Back then, plowable land was scarce to the point that a person had to plant his fields miles apart. The river must have been bigger then, because the bridge reached over the water and ten feet of land on either side of it. Some folks who moved into the area when I was a girl even called it Wabash Creek. I never could tolerate the idea that my favorite place on a warm sunny day could be anything less than a river—a water path to distant places.

Grandpa Jacob had to go and tell me it emp-tied out into a tiny duckpond about twenty miles down from the bridge. He didn't stop there. Oh no, he had to scratch the stiff whiskers on his chin as if he was trying to remember the name of someone he knew when he was young, then look me straight in the eye and say, "I don't suppose it'll be much more than a spring runoff by the time you have children, Katherine. I'd take it in while you can."

That river was a part of me. Thomas and I fished off the plow bridge every Saturday evening before supper. When he would listen, I'd read to him out of the paper. If we kept still, the fish would swim right by. I couldn't believe Grandpa's pond story when I saw those fish wiggling their way south. I trusted that the Wabash River would be there forever.

All the thoughts of fish made me hungry, so I started looking around the train car for some-one selling food. There was usually a young boy carrying his wares in a wooden box hung from his shoulders by a leather strap. In Maustone, some boy on the Chicago line usually ran over to Miss Alice's cafe for a reload as soon as the train was free of passengers. I had never even talked to one of them. They were always running at full speed as soon as they jumped off the bottom step of the train. Buford used to laugh, holding his belly as if he was afraid it was slipping farther down over his waist. "I swear those boys have the wind at their command. Haven't seen one of them slower than the wind itself."

Conductors have a way of knowing what's on a person's mind. The man conducting the train bound for Philadelphia was no exception. He came right up to the empty seat next to me and said, "Miss, if you're looking for refreshments, the dining car is just two ahead."

"Dining car?"

"Yes, that's right. They serve food, as they do in a restaurant."

"Oh yes, of course." I'd seen advertisements for them before.

He stood up nodding. "Yes, well, it's just two cars forward."

"Thank you."

He smiled and walked away. I followed his directions and came to a car filled with tables as fine as the O'Dells'. I was seated at a table with a starched linen tablecloth, clear glasses, salad forks, and napkins. My dress was wrinkled, my perfume a bit thin, but I was adorned like a lady with my barrel corset and egg-basket bustle in place. I couldn't sit square on the chair without forcing the wires of my bustle into my backside. I never bothered to wear the cumbersome thing unless I went out, so I wasn't all that practiced at sitting in it. I had to perch on the edge of the chair, and I felt like I was about to dive off a bridge for a quick swim. It was a balancing act to keep from going chest first into my plate, but I wasn't about to be discouraged by such a little thing. The prices were another story. The only thing I could afford was a fifty-cent bowl of vegetable soup. For that price, I expected them to serve it in a small pot, but the waiter brought me a wide, shallow bowl with ivy leaves etched into its rim.

The room could have come straight from my own daydreams. I was ready for my refined young gentleman to walk through the door, although I was still in battles with myself over the entire husband affair. I didn't want to seek out a man for his wallet. I wanted a companion, not a chaperon. But truth be told, I wouldn't know what to do if I attracted a suitor. I hadn't so much as talked to an unmatched man since I left Wisconsin. The last boy I had talked to was Emmet Harper, and I only spoke to him because he was standing on my shoelace in the receiving line at church.

There were the bellhops at the hotel, but they

were always rushing here and there—only stopping to steal a buttered roll off my tray or shout room-service orders from the back hallway. I never really talked to them. And if I had so much as said, "How's the weather?" to a man I was serving, Mrs. Hessmueller would have put a boot mark on my backside as she shoved me out the door.

"There will be no fraternizing with the guests!" she'd shout when she heard the waitresses discussing a customer in the hushed, giggly voices the girls in my church used to use when they discussed the local boys. I hated that sound. It reminded me too much of ducks when they herded their young.

The thought of meeting a young man sent me into a panic. My hands were sweating. I could have fainted straight away. I took deep breaths to calm myself, hoping no one noticed my foolishness. I didn't need to be frightened by the thought of meeting a man. After all, wasn't I traveling across country on my own? Didn't I make my way to Chicago? How hard could dealing with one simple man be?

It would be no different from talking to my brother Thomas. After all, he was an unmatched man. We could discuss . . . Well, I couldn't quite remember what I spoke to Thomas about besides asking him to pass the butter at dinner or telling him to get his mud-soaked boots off the floor I had just cleaned. I could ask him about his hobbies. Thomas loved to talk about the wood carvings he did of squirrels and cows. They were a bit childish actually, but the kids in church adored them.

Focusing on the idea that it would be just like talking to Thomas, I started to look forward to meeting a young man. We could talk. I could learn something new. In anticipation, I watched every man who entered the dining car and spent over an hour eating vegetable soup because I couldn't keep my mind on the meal.

I returned to my seat without so much as attracting a glance from a man. To avoid making a spectacle out of myself, I decided to take a nap. The cool glass of the window felt good against my cheek after sitting in the heat of the gas lamps in the dining car.

"Excuse me miss." The male voice was smooth like my father's when he'd carry me up to bed after I'd fallen asleep next to the fireplace.

I sat up and tried to straighten my hair before he could get a good look at me. My hair in place, I turned to answer, "Yes, sir?"

He leaned toward the empty seat beside me, hat in hand, "Is this seat taken?"

"No, sir." I tipped my chin in that direction. "Please have a seat."

"Thank you." He sat down. His jacket was made of a fine tweed. He wore a starched white collar and a satin tie. His fingernails were clean with a clear ribbon of white above his fingertips.

"Are you traveling to Philadelphia?" I asked, keeping my eyes on my own hands. The skin was dry and chapped, and my nails were cracked.

"No, miss. I get off at South Bend. I'm attending Bowling Green University."

The man next to me was a college student at a university that sounded more like a park, but it was a college nonetheless. "What are you studying there, if I may ask?"

"Certainly. I'm studying Roman history."

"Roman?" What I knew of Rome came from reading the Bible.

"Yes, the Roman Empire?" He leaned forward to see if I understood and ran his eyes over me from head to foot. I turned to the window. "Don't be offended, miss. My father hadn't even heard of Julius Caesar when I started my course work. Anyway, it's ancient history. Why would a pretty young lady like yourself need to concern yourself with such matters?"

"I'd still like to hear more about this empire you referred to." To be honest, half of me wished he would fall silent and hand me the books he'd read. I could almost smell the rich leather and musty paper of a good book as he talked. Having him sitting there, his lips moving, his voice floating around me, wasn't the same as disappearing into a book, the room around me dissolving as I drifted into another world—my own form of time travel. Such a trip wasn't possible, so I made do with his stories.

He was the first person I'd ever met who could keep smiling even while he was talking. I was beginning to wonder if his face was permanently stuck that way from smiling too much as a child. He said, "It was an empire spanning from Italy to the countries across the Mediterranean Sea. The Romans ruled the empire and Julius Caesar was their first emperor. He was assassinated in 44 B.C."

"B.C.?"

"Before Christ. The years count backward from the birth of Christ.

"Of course." I nodded, feeling foolish.

This man went from Christ to Cleopatra and tried to explain all the things that went on in a distant part of the world almost two thousand years ago. In Wisconsin, I had listened to sermons in our church. I knew that Abraham and Moses lived in an ancient time beyond my understanding, but I had never really thought about the other people who were living at the same time. While Christ suffered and died on a cross in Jerusalem, there were people in Aeslynn's Ireland called druids who worshipped the earth instead of God.

The young man was cracking open the corners of the world to show me how small Maustone, Wisconsin, really was. Not only was it a dot in comparison to the world, there were centuries surrounding it. No doubt someone had lived on the land I was born to thousands of years before me.

All the talk about the real size of the world made me think of a time when I was three and my family went on a picnic in the woods north of our house. There was a rabbit hopping between the trees, and I followed it. Thomas had sat down on a hill of biting ants, and Mother had taken him to the pond to cool the bites with fresh water. The others thought I was with her. Lord knows how long I was gone before they noticed.

The rabbit was too fast for me to keep up with, and when it bounded out of sight, I turned around to have Father chase after it for me. I remember thinking our picnic spot was right behind me. All I had to do was look over my shoulder and my family would be there. Well, they weren't. I was surrounded by towering pine trees that only let thin shafts of sunlight reach the forest floor. The lowest branches formed a canopy over my head, and as far as I could see there was a blanket of pine needles interrupted by coarse gray-brown tree trunks. The world was endless then, and I feared it.

I screamed until my family found me. My mother held me skin-tight for hours. The world shrank back to family size and I was safe. Chicago had stretched my world into a place with cities, lakes, and states. Aeslynn had introduced the concepts of countries, oceans, and continents. On a train bound for Philadelphia, I was discovering the past. I found myself gripping the handle on Edith's suitcase until the rope burned my hand.

"An old suitcase you have there. Your grandmother's?"

"No." I shook my head.

"Heavens, I'm not going to steal it from you."

"Oh." I let go and put my hands in my lap. "Sorry, I'm just a little nervous."

"Where on earth are my manners?" He shook his head. "I haven't even introduced myself. My name is Harlan Wilson." He offered a hand.

It was soft like my own cheek. I held it a bit too long. He blushed, then took his hand away in laughter. "Sorry," I said as a smile spread across my face to hide my embarrassment. "Nice to meet you, Mr. Wilson."

"Harlan, please. And you are?"

"My name's Edith Shay."

"Now that's a pretty name."

"Thank you."

"Well, I've gone on enough about college. What about you? Where are you headed?"

"You wouldn't be interested. What will you do once you finish college?"

"Teach." He nodded. "Of course some men go on for a degree in law."

"To be a lawyer?" I thought back to my day-dreams of marrying a man who would travel the country with me at his side—an itinerant lawyer who traveled through the lawless lands of the frontier would do just that. I smiled.

"That's right." He smiled. "My father has always wanted me to try for a law degree, but the exams are insurmountable. Don't let me dwell on myself." He shifted in his seat to face me. "Excuse me for being forward, but . . ."

The conductor passed our seat in a rush, heading for the front of the car. I watched him walk up to a young boy who had just stepped into the car. He was a sandwich boy selling his wares. I was suddenly hungry for butter and salt pork on homemade bread. I started searching through my purse to find enough coins to pay for the sandwich.

The conductor was grumbling at the sandwich boy. He probably didn't want the boy to lure the first-class customers away from the dining car where they charged fifty cents for a bowl of soup. I moved to leave the seat before the conductor shooed the boy away, saying, "Could you excuse me?"

"What do you need?" When I turned to answer Harlan, he wasn't looking at my face; his eyes were on my open purse.

"I was hungry for a sandwich." I pointed over the seat to the conductor.

"I'll get one for you." Harlan smiled. "What kind of gentleman would I be if I didn't pay for the meals of a woman in my company?"

A dirt poor one, as far as I could see. When he fished his coin purse out of his pocket, it was no bigger than a dollar piece. He stepped into the aisle and walked right in front of the conductor to get a sandwich. The boy held one out, and after a quick look in his coin purse, Harlan started digging in his pockets. So much for chivalry.

He returned with the sandwich. "Here you are. I hope you don't mind salt pork. It makes my mouth dry."

"I love it," I said, unwrapping the sandwich. The sandwich was good, but it made me drowsy.

Harlan started talking about gladiators and lead pipes, and I couldn't keep my eyes open. I hummed a bit here and there to let him know I was listening, and he kept chattering away. It wasn't long before I felt myself slipping off to sleep.

When I woke up, Harlan wasn't there. I sat up to look around. I didn't feel the familiar tug of my purse around my waist, so I searched my seat. Panicking didn't help me find it, but it brought the conductor. "Can I help you, miss?"

"I can't find my purse!" I was facing my seat as I searched the car for Harlan.

The conductor leaned forward and lifted something off the floor. "This look familiar to you, miss?" He held up the satin cords to my purse. I pulled the cords away from him, still too slow to understand what had happened.

"Miss, that young man you were sitting with has robbed you. I should have known he was up to no good when he got off before the stop on his ticket."

"Robbed me?" I dropped to my seat in a stupor; then I remembered Edith's suitcase. I sat forward so abruptly that I hit my head on the seat in front of me, but the suitcase was safely tucked beneath me. I pulled it out and searched inside to be sure he hadn't taken anything. All of

Edith's things were still there. I didn't know what to do. I was stuck on that train. I couldn't chase him and who knew what I'd do if I could. I had no money. No one to call on in Philadelphia. I could do nothing but worry.

The only thing I noticed about the station in Philadelphia was the noise. It could have been a henhouse full of chickens for all I knew. I was penniless. After Chicago, I knew what being penniless in a new city meant.

It meant peddling myself door to door to find a room and board for the night. A search for a job would follow, and I'd be held down like a bird with salt on its tail until I could raise enough money for a ticket to Washington. I was smart enough to know there weren't two Aeslynn O'Dells in the world.

I was standing on the street corner across from the station before I was even aware of my surroundings. The ticky-tap of the telegraph office pulled me up short. I thought of wiring Aeslynn to send some help. I considered wiring a plea to my parents to forgive me and send a ticket home. The fear of making my way in Philadelphia collided head-on with my shame at the thought of running back to my elders at the first sign of trouble.

I stood there on the brick street crying like a foolish child lost in the crowd at a fair. It wasn't long before I started to attract attention. Women walking shoulder to shoulder on the boardwalk paused to point and whisper to each other. Children stopped their play to stare. I saw these things because I wasn't ashamed enough to cover my eyes. A lady in a navy-blue hat garnished with a dried daisy walked up to me. "Miss, are you all right? Do you need help?"

I was a blubbering fool. When I opened my mouth, tiny squeals came out. The woman took my elbow and patted me on the shoulder with her free hand, "There, there now. You come inside here, out of the cold." She escorted me into a shop filled with odd, thresherlike machinery, then brought me to a back room. Offering me a seat on a bench, she sat down beside me.

"Now, miss, you have to calm down." She was still patting my shoulder. I was reminded of the way the cow's tail used to catch me on the shoulder while I was milking her.

"I'm sorry," I blubbered as I opened the suitcase to find a handkerchief.

"Here." She handed me one from her sleeve. "It's fresh."

"Thank you." I nodded, wiping my nose.

"Now, what's your problem?"

"I was robbed."

"Robbed?" She jumped up from the bench and turned to face me. "We need to notify the constable right away."

"It didn't happen here."

"Where then?"

"On the train."

"Oh." She sat down. "That's dreadful. At least they didn't take your suitcase."

"No, but they took my money."

"Don't tell me you kept all your money in one place?"

"My purse."

"Never, never keep all your money in one place, child."

"Yes, ma'am."

"Well, there's no reason to tear up over it. Money doesn't grow on trees, but it doesn't pave your way to Heaven either."

I was too busy worrying about my problem to hear her advice. I started talking even before she got her last word out. "I was going to get off the train in Philadelphia and buy a ticket for Washington."

"Oh, dear." Stray hairs fell out of her bun as she shook her head. "This is quite serious. Do you have any kin in Philadelphia?"

"Not that I know of."

"Dear." She looked from left to right as if a solution was sitting on one of the shelves which surrounded us. Her glances made me look around. I realized I was in a room filled with books. It wasn't a library, and yet there were shelves full of books.

"Are these all yours?" I stood up and ran my fingers over the bindings.

"Yes," she answered in confusion.

"How can you afford so many books?" I started to read the titles, admiring the pressed letters and the contrasting ink which had been used to dye them.

"This is a print shop." She stood up. "We make books."

"You make books?" I had thought they were produced by robed figures in shadowy rooms, Lord knows why. I didn't know a printing press from a loom, so I had no idea the machinery we passed when we walked in made books.

"Yes." She took a step closer to me. "You suddenly seem more interested in our books than your predicament."

"Oh, I am." I turned to face her. "I love books. I could spend my life in a library."

"Well, you may have to, if you don't find a way to get yourself back home. Where is home for you?"

The word *home* made me feel hollow inside. I'd lost mine and was hoping I'd find a new one with Edith Shay. "I'm heading for Virginia."

"Virginia? That's no place for a young woman to be traveling to."

"I need to return something to a friend of mine."

"I see." Her face tightened. "Then why did you say you were only in Philadelphia to buy a ticket to Washington?"

"I have to go to Washington to buy a ticket on a southern line to take me into Richmond."

"Richmond?" She slapped her chest with an open palm. "Are you out of your mind?"

I couldn't understand why she was so shocked, so I answered her with half a question. "No?"

"Richmond is nothing but a hole in the ground, child. We bombed those Rebels to Kingdom Come."

I couldn't imagine a city being reduced to a hole in the ground. There wasn't anything on earth that could eat up all those buildings. I knew from the papers that the Union soldiers had pushed the residents of Richmond into the cave outside the city, but I figured five years was plenty of time to rebuild what had been destroyed in the war. "I suppose that's true, but it's been five years."

"Well, anyone with enough sense to come in out of a storm would have left that city years ago. If this thing you're returning is so valuable you have to carry it all the way to Virginia, I'd carry it in something a little more protective than that battered old suitcase of yours. It looks like it went through the Battle of Five Forks itself."

"Yes, ma'am." I noticed I'd left one of the seals unlatched, so I closed it up, then turned to face her. "I thank you so much for taking me in like you did. I just wasn't sure what direction to turn. I won't bother you anymore."

"Wait a minute now." She took my elbow to keep me from walking out. "What direction did you decide on, being penniless and a long way from Richmond?"

"I'll look for a job and save up for a ticket to Washington."

"Well, you go sit yourself down on the bench outside. I'll have a word with my husband and see what he can do for you."

"Oh no, ma'am. You don't have to do that."

"I know. I could be digging my own grave by pulling you in off the street, but the Bible says treat every stranger like an angel lest he be one."

"Yes, ma'am."

"Well, get out there."

The bench outside was occupied by two old

men comparing watches, so I leaned against the front wall of the shop and set the suitcase down at my feet. It seemed near to impossible that a crying fit on a street could lead to a job, but it was happening. There are rare moments in life when there's no possible reason for things to happen as they do and you have to see God's hand in the matter. After all God wouldn't leave me penniless and crying on the street in January.

A man leaned out of the doorway of the print shop, his narrow face flushed red. "Miss, come inside."

"Yes, sir." I bowed my head, then stepped in.

The man was already on his way to the back of the shop. For a moment, I had the idea that he was racing against me. His legs were moving so fast, the laces on his shoes were in constant flight. His urgency pushed me to go quicker and I caught up to him just as he was turning into a dimly lit office. To my surprise, I saw right over his shoulder. My view of his wife's face was unobstructed. I could see every twist in her look of concern. The man had to be a head under my five feet and two inches in height.

"Now." He sat down behind his desk. I couldn't help but notice that the pockets of his vest were visible above the surface of the desk. "What's your name, young lady?"

"Edith Shay." It rolled off my tongue as naturally as saying my ABCs.

"To complete the formalities, my name is Lawford Denison." He touched his chest with an open palm, then motioned toward his wife with the same hand. "This is my wife Vivian."

"I'm pleased to know you both." I stood by the door with my head bent to keep myself from staring at the tiny man.

"You were robbed on the train?"

"Yes, sir."

"My wife seems to think we should accept you into our lives as a token of charity. I think you're a charlatan looking to take advantage of our generosity. What have you to say in your own defense?"

"I have said nothing that isn't the strictest truth since I got here, sir." I had to look him in the eye to gain his trust. Aeslynn had taught me that. It wasn't until I saw the cold, doubting look in his eyes that I realized I had lied. I'd said my name was Edith Shay! Heavens, at the time, I'd simply said it without thinking. I barely remembered I wasn't her after all those months of using her name, but it was no time to panic. I had to convince him that I could be trusted, if not by speaking the absolute truth, then because of his generosity. "If you feel the need to prove my story, you could speak with the conductor on the five o'clock train from Chicago. He saw the man who committed the crime."

"I see." He turned away and shifted some of the paperwork on his desk. "If you wish to work for us to make up for your lost resources, you'll have to give us some collateral."

"Collateral?"

"That's right. You'll have to give us something of yours that we can keep. Something valuable enough to keep you from running off with our cash box in the middle of the night."

"All I have is what I'm taking to Virginia."

"If it's valuable enough to be delivered in person across so many miles, it must be worth a pretty penny."

"I couldn't put a price on it, sir, but it means a lot to me."

"That settles it, then. Vivian, take her suitcase." He shook his hand at his wife to send her into action. She rushed across the room and grabbed the case without even glancing at me.

A tingling sensation covered the skin of my palms as she pulled the suitcase away. For a moment, I thought I could float. I felt so empty without it.

"This is a family-run business. There's Vivian and myself as well as a few young fellows who set the type. Having someone to clean up would free Vivian to do more important things. I expect you to arrive here every weekday morning at nine without fail or you will lose the job on the spot. I'm willing to accept mistakes, but only once. Keep that in mind, young lady, because I won't be romanced into giving you a second chance."

"Yes, sir."

"I will give you a letter of recommendation for the boarding house down the street. The woman is a family friend. She will probably take you in if you have good domestic skills." He pulled a clean sheet of paper out of a pile on his desk, then took up an ink pen.

"Thank you, sir."

"Your gratitude should be reflected in the quality of your work. The pay is forty-five cents a day, not a penny more!" He slapped the desk to punctuate his announcement, and his chair shook. There was a twinge of panic that tightened the skin around his eyes as it wobbled, then he bent over the paper to write the letter. "My wife will lock the suitcase in our safe after you leave. You will get it upon your departure. I expect at least a two-week resignation notice."

"Yes, sir."

"The boarding house is a chicken-beak yellow house in the middle of the next block. You'll know it by the weathered sign hanging from the front porch. Mrs. Rayburn runs the place. She's a widow with a soft spot for drifters who can stomach her cooking."

"Mrs. Rayburn's a personal friend of mine. A nice lady," Vivian whispered without looking up.

"I'm sure she is. A church-going woman," Lawford added, blotting the letter, then folding it. "Here you are."

I stepped forward to take the letter and couldn't help but take a glance down to see what he was sitting on. He must have seen me, because his cheeks flushed red as he yelled, "Be here by nine! Now, get out!"

"Thank you, sir." I rushed out of the office. As soon as I cleared the doorway, the Denisons started bickering. I was moving too fast to hear it all but the words "stranger," "privacy," and "profit" caught my ear as I was making my way to the door.

The weight of the arrangement came over me as I stepped into the street. I'd given those people power over my livelihood. They had everything I owned, and control over what I could do. I had the urge to rush back into the shop and demand to have my suitcase back. Something told me they wouldn't return it if I did, so I walked down the block, praying I'd put my trust in the right people.

Tested by Fire

———✦———

Walking down the street in search of the boarding house, I realized that Philadelphia was full of history. The saloon across the street was called a tavern. It had the year 1798 inscribed over the doorway. The brick walls had been whitewashed, and they had a foggy quality to them under the fine white powder. The house next door was a stout box with deep blue shutters and flower boxes at every window. The street wasn't a packed-down strip of dirt. It was a brick wall laid into the ground. Each brick had been placed by hand, and the city of Philadelphia was laced with brick streets.

The approach of a box coach startled me into continuing my search for the boarding house.

The house I found with a wooden sign hanging from the porch was river-water blue. It was newly painted and the sign was hung a bit crooked. I tapped on the front door, hoping that I wasn't disturbing the wrong person. Through the window in the door, I could see someone approaching. The face was angular, with high cheekbones, a pointed chin, and an L-shaped jaw. I was certain it belonged to a man, until she opened the door and I saw it was a woman's.

The woman smiled, pushing curves into her face. "Good evening, can I help you?"

"Yes, thank you. My name's Edith Shay. I've come by recommendation from the Denisons."

She took the letter I offered and tucked it into her apron, "You don't need any recommendation to stay in my home, miss."

"I don't have any money to pay for a room."

"Now that's a little different." She stepped to the side. "Come in."

I walked inside. The parlor was visible from the hallway. The wooden fireplace was painted white. There was a dark oil painting over the mantel of a stern-looking man holding a book to his chest. The furniture was well kept, but unpolished. The room didn't have the distant expensive feel of the O'Dell home—it was warm and inviting like my own.

"Miss Shay, I'm Doreen Rayburn." She offered a hand. Her grip was firm and callused. "I've run this place for the last twenty years, since my husband died. He still keeps his eye on the place." She nodded toward the painting. "Don't be fooled by the glum look or his acquaintance with Lawford Denison. He was a gentle old man."

"Yes, ma'am."

"Can you cook?"

"I worked for the Greymore Hotel in Chicago as a night cook."

"If you were a night cook, chances are they were too drunk to notice." She started to make her way down the hall, then motioned for me to follow. "I don't allow alcohol in this house. My husband and I have a good Christian home."

"Yes, ma'am."

"You'll cook dinner tonight. If you're good, then you'll be responsible for it six days a week. Sundays we rest. The guests can eat what's cold and fresh from the icebox."

"Yes, ma'am."

"I hope you've got more than 'yes' to say for yourself, young lady. Around here you'd better have a quick tongue and a sure sense of yourself if you intend to fend for your own livelihood."

"Yes, ma'am."

She laughed and stepped into the kitchen. "You have two hours before dinner needs to be served. I won't so much as lift a finger, but I'll keep the fact that this kitchen is new to you in mind. There will be fourteen at the table including me and you. We'll talk after the meal is finished."

The meal, as she called it, was a coal-fire test of my intelligence. Fourteen was eight more than I'd ever served at one time without help. My first step was to take stock of everything Mrs. Rayburn had in her kitchen. She actually had more pans and spices than the Greymore. She didn't have the fresh produce they were so proud of, but then again the hotel couldn't boast fresh cream or milk. Theirs was sometimes as much as a day old because they had to wait for deliveries from Lake Forest or Elgin. Once I had an idea of the raw materials available, I set out to make potato pie with pork shoulder and garden vegetables. I covered the kitchen with a fine layer of flour as I struggled to make enough crust for three pies. Three's not a tall order of pies unless you have pork shoulder in the oven, vegetables to shuck, cut, and clean, milk to skim, and muffins to prepare for dessert.

Voices started to fill the dining room as I took the pies out of the oven. I was struck with the

idea that I had to serve the meal as well. I had
no idea where the service dishes were nor the
table settings. When I peered into the dining
room, I noticed that Mrs. Rayburn had already
set the table. With one obstacle out of the way, I
searched for the service dishes with such frantic
need that I forgot about the muffins. They
burned to the point of resembling wood tar, and
I had to resort to my mother's raw cinnamon
rolls. I buttered twenty-eight slices of bread,
sprinkled them with cinnamon sugar and a
touch of nutmeg, then sandwiched them. I flattened each sandwich with a rolling pin, then
whirled them up into tiny logs. Flattening them
again, I added a little syrup, then rolled them
into little wheels. They looked like a plate of
raw sausages busting out of their skins.

Mrs. Rayburn called into the kitchen without
looking through the doorway, "Miss Shay, I
hope you're about ready. We have hungry guests
ready to eat."

"Yes, ma'am."

"Yes, ma'am," she echoed as she returned to
the dining room.

Dinner was served and everyone sat in silence
as they stared down at their bare plates. My potato
pie slices didn't take up more than a quarter of
the plate. The vegetables had grown cold, and

the cinnamon rolls were an obvious disgrace. I kept my head bowed and my plate empty.

"New cook, Mrs. Rayburn?" asked a man at the far end of the table.

"That's right, Mr. Shultz. Don't be shy, gentlemen, your response determines her future here."

Their stares covered my shoulders with a sheet of ice. I pulled my muscles tight to keep from shivering, and clasped my hands in my lap. Everyone ate in silence. Some men excused themselves from the table in a matter of minutes. The entire meal was over before the grandfather clock in the corner struck at the half-hour. Mrs. Rayburn didn't speak until after the last guest left. She waited another minute, then cleared her throat to say, "Miss Shay, look at me."

I lifted my head. Her harsh face was pressed into a soft, rounded smile that pulled on the tight gray bun on her head. "That's better. Now, how do you feel about this meal?"

"It was a miserable failure."

"Adequately phrased." She folded her napkin and placed it on her empty plate. "You didn't cook enough food, you let it get cold, and you didn't prepare adequately for a dessert."

"Yes, ma'am."

"Do you have anything to say in your defense?"

Excuses spun through my head. I was robbed.

I'm only sixteen. I've never cooked for such a large group before. I didn't know the kitchen. I've never worked with the stove before. I pushed them all to the side and said, "No ma'am."

"Well, there's a change. I was wondering what it would take to get you to say no. Most girls I bring in here never even get their meals to the table. Last one dumped her main dish on my head. That was one time I was glad someone had let her food get cold."

I bit my lip to hold back a laugh.

"Oh, go ahead, laugh." She tapped the table. "God can already hear you. Your room is the first door on the right when you go up the back stairs. You can go to bed as soon as you make another helping of that delicious pie for everyone. Make it hot." She stood up. "Bring it to their rooms and clean up that abominable mess you made in my kitchen!" She walked away without so much as a glance in my direction.

It was past midnight before I threw the dish-water over the flower garden and blew out the lamp to go upstairs to bed. The back stairs wound up from the kitchen and each step was no deeper than my feet were long. I expected my room to be as tight and uncomfortable. On the contrary, it was my room over Aeslynn's shop all over again. I had my own bed, which was stuffed

with feathers not straw, a washstand, and a
dresser. The boarding-house room even had a
closet with its own door and shelves. There was
also a low seat in front of the window. When I
sat down, I could see out to a courtyard in front
of a brick building with a clock tower. No one
was about at the witching hour, so the shadows
of the barren bushes on the snow made me think
of nighttime spirits. I pulled down the shades and
slipped into bed, still clothed.

I listened to the house settle—the distant moans
and creaks made me think of Father sneaking
down to have a cup of nighttime tea. Ever since
his days on the railroad, he had trouble sleeping
through the night. Back when he and his brothers
were building bridges and sleeping under the
trestles for protection against the wind, it was
the fear of cave-ins that woke him. At home, it
had become a habit.

"It's a wonderful time to watch the frost form
on the windows or the dew bud on the grass,"
Father used to say when I found him standing
in front of a window, a teacup in his hand.

I closed my eyes and prayed I'd find my
father standing at the window when I opened
them, but I didn't deserve such a miracle. The
room was still bare when I looked. I had to find
a way to touch my family, tell them what I was

feeling. Using the wrapping from my salt pork sandwich, I wrote them a letter.

January 3, 1870

Dear Family,

It's hard to believe the new year has come. This last one has been too painful for us all, I think. I miss you and Wisconsin more each day. I know I should return. I promise that I will. But my journey would be for naught if I don't see it through. Perhaps I'm chasing after nonsense, but I need to find a life for myself.

Please understand, the life you gave me was grand, more than most girls could hope for, but you gave it so freely. I didn't deserve it. Like Father, Grandpa Jacob, and Grandpa Vince, I want to work for what is mine, build something I can call my own.

Know that I love you and I miss you dearly. Please forgive me.

The letter finished, I folded it, then slid it under my pillow. I cursed myself for not waiting for a reply in Chicago. If I wanted to be so brave and do things on my own, why hadn't I faced what my family had to say to me? I knew then that I should have told Aeslynn where I was going, let her know a letter would be coming from my parents.

Ah, but the letter would have been addressed to Katherine Lunden, and who was that to Aeslynn O'Dell? I had certainly made a mess of things, but I was too tired to work them all out that night.

The tolling of the clock in the tower pulled me out of bed the next morning. I mistook it for the steam whistle and feared for my father's life. When I came to my senses and realized that the clock had tolled more than eight times, I panicked. I was halfway down the front steps when Mrs. Rayburn called after me from her bedroom window, "Child, where are you going?"

"I'm late for work!"

"Work?" Mrs. Rayburn laughed. Her laughter reminded me of the sound apples made in the wooden barrel when we rolled it up to the house after a day of picking. "It's Saturday, child. Denison's shop isn't open today. He spends his Saturdays selling his stock to booksellers."

I dropped right down on the steps and laughed until I couldn't breathe. Every stupid thing I'd done in the last three days came tumbling back as a big joke; leaving Aeslynn, trusting Harlan, giving my suitcase to Mr. Denison, making raw cinnamon rolls for dessert. Mrs. Rayburn appeared in the doorway. "I can't see how getting your days mixed up could be all that funny."

"It isn't. I was just thinking that I should try and give myself a little dignity by washing up and changing clothes, and I realized I gave all my clothes to Mr. Denison."

"And that's funny?"

"No, it's so darn stupid, I had to laugh."

"I see." She pulled her shawl closer over her shoulders. "There was a time when I wasn't as wide as a four-post bed. For sentimental reasons, I kept the clothes I wore back then. I see no reason why you can't wear them. They aren't fancy like that one you have on, but they'll keep you warmer. That one looks like it collects more snow than it keeps out."

"I'd be so grateful, but you're too generous."

"The Lord says be generous to all strangers because any one of them could be an angel."

I laughed. "I'm no angel."

"Maybe so." She squeezed my hand. "I do know you're what my husband would call honey in water. You've got enough in you to keep your sweetness together, but it's only a matter of time before it dissolves under pressure."

"Excuse me?"

"In plain English that means you've got a lot of spunk, but spunk can get you only so far in this world."

"Thank you."

"Thank me by getting inside before you catch your death and I have to find another cook."

I followed her inside, then upstairs to her room. She gripped her skirts, then lowered herself down to the floor in front of a steamer trunk. "This was a wedding present from my husband's brother. Heavens, it seems like it was a century ago."

She pushed the lid open and ran her fingers over the quilt inside. "I sewed this when I was thirteen years old. We lived in the grist mill my father ran in Gifford, Pennsylvania. My mother never left my side, because she didn't trust the boys who came in with their fathers to have their grain run through the mill. My father laughed at her, saying that they were more likely to mistake me for a son than a daughter." Doreen noticed the deep frown on my face and smiled. "Oh, I knew how plain I was.

"When I was close to marrying age, my parents thought to send me to a convent, but they weren't devoutly religious folk and didn't like the thought of me being kept away from the rest of the world. Instead, they made a contract with a hospital here in Philadelphia. The one you see out the back door. I did laundry six days a week and got room and board. The hospital sent my parents ten dollars a month.

"There was a doctor who had me do his own laundry. He saw me collecting sheets one night and asked my name. Next thing I knew, he'd brought out his laundry. He looked so old to me. With the wisps of hair on his head and the crimped-up skin around his eyes, he looked like my grandfather. He didn't say much to me, but he was always smiling and he gave me a penny for every shirt I washed.

"He asked about my father one afternoon. Wondered where he was and how he felt about marriage. I told him where my parents lived and said they enjoyed being married very much. He laughed at me, and I didn't know why until he brought me a daisy the next day. He sat me down on the chair by the laundry bin and put the flower in my hand, then said, 'Doreen, I may be an old man, but I know a good person when I see one. You are a good person.'

"I tried to thank him, but he covered my lips with his soft fingertips. 'A good person deserves happiness. I would like the opportunity to give you your happiness.'

"I didn't quite realize he was asking for my hand in marriage until he presented me with the ring." She held out her hand to show me the gold band on her finger.

"That doctor was my husband, Mason Rayburn. It was three days after my fourteenth birthday when I walked down that aisle. I was a little slip of a thing, like you." She touched my hand. "Don't be shocked dear, I meant my body shape. You've got a beautiful face. Such white skin, it's like God carved you out of ice."

"You're too kind." I blushed.

"Make that clay, you're as red as the blood in my veins."

I smiled, saying, "Tell me more."

She opened her mouth to speak, then laughed. She gripped my knee and asked, "Child, what do you have inside you that's got me talking about my life as if you were my own flesh and blood? I've just been babbling on."

"My grandmother Margaret used to say you can't tell the ones you love a thing because they know you well enough to judge you by it. Strangers don't know you, and they're rarely around long enough to hold anything against you."

"Smart woman." Mrs. Rayburn nodded, then rubbed the quilt. "I was pregnant before I turned sixteen. I had a son. It wasn't an easy birth. I near about died. My husband was so afraid of losing me, he kept filling me with food to weight me down to earth. That's how I widened out."

"I raised my boy in this house. After his father

died, I took in boarders to pay the bills. Now he's a professor at George Washington University, in Washington City."

"I'm going to Washington," I pointed out.

"Are you really? Tell me you're not lying?"

"I'm not."

"Then you'll have to take some things for my grandchildren with you. I can't help but buy them things all year round, then my son accuses me of spoiling them." She started digging her way through the clothes packed into the trunk. "I must have dresses in here somewhere."

"I'm sorry about your husband. He sounds like he was such a nice man."

"A saint, I tell you. He was sixty-three years old when he married me. He near about had a stroke when he found out he was going to be a father. He was happy and scared all at the same time. When I was sickly after Richard was born, he was so worried I'd die, and then our son would be an orphan, because his father was sure to die of old age before he reached maturity. Mason was right. His heart quit on him when Richard was fifteen years old.

"Richard was so bitter that a fellow doctor couldn't save his father, he swore off the medical profession and went to school to be a philosophy professor."

"Philosophy?"

"I don't pretend to understand philosophy myself. It's something about ways of thinking handed down from generations past. All too bookish for me. Give me a good Bible and I'm set for life." She pulled a brown cotton dress from the trunk. "Here we are. Wrinkled and maybe a bit long, but a dandy just the same."

"Thank you." I took the dress and folded it into my lap. "I'll return it before I leave."

Mrs. Rayburn laughed. "What for, child? I'm not going to wear it."

"Thank you."

"Girl, you are a two-word woman. You hardly ever say more than two words at a time. What else have you got to say for yourself?"

I wasn't about to bore her with my own life. Instead, I wanted to know more about hers. "I have nothing to compare to that story."

The clock in the tower struck. "My goodness, it's eleven, child, we've got a meal to prepare. I let you sleep through breakfast, but you need to help me with lunch."

"I'd be glad to."

"I should think so. You have a lot to learn if you're going to be feeding my guests on a daily basis."

Truth was, I had a lot to learn on every subject.

What Can You Do?

———◆———

I arrived in front of the glass doors of Denison's print ship at exactly 8:45 on Monday morning. I could see a clock on the back wall. I waited patiently at the locked glass doors, watching the images of the people walking behind me wobble across the polished glass. Lawford Denison passed through the hallway in the back of the shop to enter his office. I knew for a fact that I was visible from that distance. I could see my own reflection in the mirror on his open office door. He didn't even look up. At nine o'clock, he emerged from his office, checked his watch, then came to open the front door.

"Good morning, Miss Shay. Have the floor scrubbed before ten A.M. We open our doors on the hour and my customers expect to see a shine. The materials are over there." He returned to his office in silence.

I found a bucket of water on the counter with a bar of soap, scrub brush, and drying rag. Grabbing the broom from the corner, I swept the floor. The clouds of dust that rose from the floor were black with ink. There was no dust-pan in sight, so I swept the inky dust into the street. The people on the boardwalk stepped down into the street to avoid the clouds of ink.

As I came back into the shop, Mrs. Denison leaned out of the doorway across from the office. She checked to see that her husband wasn't watching, then turned to me and whispered, "Miss Shay, I will bring your clothes to Doreen's after the evening meal. If you need more water, there's a well pump out back. You can come through here to use the back door."

"Thank you," I whispered in return.

She disappeared without a response. I started to scrub in the far southwest corner of the shop and worked my way across the floor. When I placed my hand on the floor to brace myself, I could feel a greasy film that the broom hadn't touched. My skirts soaked up as much of the slimy dirt as the scrub brush. The ink residue under the machines swirled under the brush, but it wouldn't come off the floor except to stain my dress. I blamed it on the water and went to change it.

When I returned, Mr. Denison was standing in the spot I had actually finished. "What are you doing?" His head was held at such an angle it looked like he was having trouble keeping it on his neck. He gripped his hips with his forefingers and thumbs.

"I'm scrubbing the floor."

He pointed to the drying rag on the counter. "Did the idea ever occur to you to wipe up the ink with a rag before you scrubbed?"

"No, sir."

"Might I remind you, young lady, I hired you out of the kindness of my heart. I suggest you put some effort into doing your job the proper way. Every educated person on this earth knows you can't clean ink with water and soap alone. Not to mention the simple fact that every floor is washed from the east side to the west side. Every good Christian knows that you follow the path of the Lord's design. The sun rises in the east and sets in the west. Now finish this mess!" He stomped back to the office. I was struck by the fact that his feet sounded like my brother Thomas when he used to be sent to the corner for spilling his milk. Denison leaned into the hall to add, "You won't be paid for today's work, because we'll have to open late on account of your stupidity."

Mr. Denison's reprimand hollowed me. He was right. Wiping the floor first was a matter of common sense, yet it hadn't crossed my mind. I thought the rag was for drying the darn floor. Who dries their floor anyway? The rag took up a good share of the ink from the floor, and the residue came up with soap and water. I scrambled to finish the work on time, but I didn't dump my last bucket of water until ten-fifteen.

Mr. Denison rushed out of his office to open the doors. I expected to see a stream of people come in, but no one did. The people passing by didn't even look in. On his way back to his office he said, "You'll take your lunch break now. Get home and get out of those filthy clothes!" He gripped the knob of his office door, then turned to say, "Be back by eleven sharp and have the good sense God gave you to wear an apron!"

I felt like such a fool as I walked back to the boarding house. My dress was a complete disgrace, and it wasn't even mine. I feared what Mrs. Rayburn would have to say when she saw me. After all her generosity, I'd gone and destroyed the dress she loaned to me. She was standing at the sink peeling carrots when I came in the back door.

"What on earth?"

"I'm so sorry," I blurted, trying to cover the stains with my hands, like a child.

"Is Denison so tight-fisted with his money that he'd rather make you scrub the floor with your dress than buy a decent mop?"

Bowing my head, I said, "I didn't know enough to wipe up the ink before I scrubbed the floor."

Mrs. Rayburn nodded. "I see." Wiping her hands on her apron, she took a large tin bowl from a hook on the wall. "Fill this with water and orange slices. We might be able to save the dress."

"Yes, ma'am." I did as I was told.

"Yes, ma'am. Yes, ma'am." Mrs. Rayburn sang as I pumped water. I couldn't keep from laughing, and she joined me. "You certainly are a peach, Miss Shay!"

Taking an orange from the window cooler, I said, "Are you sure you want to waste an orange on the dress? I could buy you a new one." In Wisconsin, an orange in winter was a rare treat.

"With what?" Mrs. Rayburn laughed. "No, child. An orange is a lot cheaper than a new dress."

I caught myself before I answered with a "Yes, ma'am."

Cutting the orange, I thought of my own

mother. I remembered the time I got my dress caught on a barbed-wire fence when I went hunting for pheasant eggs with Thomas. Mother was so angry, she wouldn't speak to me for a week. I had to sew up the tear and wear that dress until it was threadbare and an inch too short because, as Mother said, "Good dresses don't grow on trees."

I felt like wearing a burlap sack every time Mother said that, but thinking back on it made me miss her. It also reminded me of the letter I'd written on Friday night. Dropping the oranges into the bowl, I ran upstairs to grab the letter and change my clothes. If I hurried, I could get to the post office before my lunch break was over.

When I returned to work after mailing the letter, Mr. Denison set me down in the back corner of the shop with a bottle of rubbing alcohol and a pile of wooden boxes filled with hundreds of steel-cast letters. He had three young men with hunched shoulders and greasy faces who spent their days bent over similar boxes picking out the letters to place into printing sleds in the order they were supposed to appear on the pages of a book. I had to clean the letters to ensure there was no ink build-up that would make the letters unreadable. I held each letter between my fingertips, then used a cotton swab dipped in alcohol to remove all the visible ink.

At first, I daydreamed about the books those letters would make—bound in leather, filling polished wooden shelves in private libraries, telling tales of grand adventures: riding a stagecoach through a desert no-man's-land, braving the raging Colorado river on a raft, surviving a cruel Nebraska winter in a soddy. But after a few hours of the tedious, finger-stretching routine, I was too tired to dream.

Instead, I thought of a way to speed things up. I rinsed out the bucket I used to clean the floor, then filled the bottom with alcohol. I dropped a box full of letters into the bucket. I removed them one by one and wiped them down. After a good soak, the ink came off with ease. Some of the letters came out of the bucket clean as a silver spoon after a good polish. I went through a box in less than two hours and was quite proud of my new method until Mr. Denison interrupted his proofreading to check on my progress.

"Are you insane?" He shook the bucket. "These letters cost a fortune. You can't soak them. You'll destroy the backing!" He dumped the bucket onto the counter and sent the letters skittering across the table, the clear alcohol gushing over the edge. "Clean this up and come into my office."

I dried off each letter and put them into a box. I wanted to do it perfectly so that I could keep the job. I had to show him I could do it right.

"Miss Shay, I have noticed that you don't possess a keen sense of intelligence, so I'd appreciate it if you don't make any decisions on your own. If you are told to do something, do it the way you were told to."

"Yes, sir." I bowed my head.

"That's enough for today." He started occupying himself with the papers on his desk. "Come back tomorrow. Be here at eight and wash the floor."

"Yes, sir."

Walking home, my last mistake echoed in my head, and Mr. Denison's shouts pounded in my temples. I didn't want to give that man the satisfaction of haunting my thoughts, so I forced myself to fill my mind with other things. Take for instance the houses along the street. Each building had a tint of gray in the cold of that winter afternoon. In Chicago, I had seen what they called a townhouse, but the ones in Philadelphia had a unique way about them— little windows that poked out of the roof like the eyes of a frog, or peculiarly shaped stones over the doorway that reminded me of worn-down

arrowheads with the points facing the stoops. I
later learned they were called keystones and
were a sign of good luck—Pennsylvania's version
of a horseshoe hung over a barn door. And I still
marveled at all the brick and stone they used to
make their buildings. Some houses even had
little stone plaques along the roofline carved
with flourishes or flowers. They were pleasant
to the eye but too nearly akin to a tombstone for
my pleasure. Back home, buildings were made
of wood, but in Philadelphia they saved their
wood for massive, carved doors that made each
home look like it was ready to receive a king or
queen.

I got so caught up in my study of the houses
along the street that I was afraid I'd be late getting back to Mrs. Rayburn's. Luckily, I reached
her place in time to refuel the stove for supper. I
made dessert first to be sure that I had it right. I
decided on cake, because I had become a master
at frosting. Even if it wasn't the lightest cake, it
would be the prettiest. Beef stew was my choice
for a main course, and I made enough to fill a
two-gallon pot. It bubbled on the stove as I sat
down on a stool to frost the cake. Pushing the
creamy confection into tiny peaks warmed me
up from the inside out. It was something I could
do and do well. When I was through, I sat up to

call my mother to have her come see what I had done. I had my lips formed around the word when I realized she wasn't there to be called. I had to take a deep breath to keep from crying.

I put my hand in the flour dust on the counter, then raised it to my face to smell it. When I was a child and my mother would bake, I'd watch her from the bench by the window as I played with the wooden blocks Father had carved. She'd sit down beside me with a spoon in her hand for me to lick. I liked her corn muffin mix the best. My mouth made more spit to soak it all up. Mother would pull me into her lap, then help me name the letters on my block while she waited for the cake to bake or the muffins to rise. I could hear her soothing voice and smell the flour. Mother used it so much, I could smell it in her clothes when I took them outside to do the washing.

The memory of her made me ache to see her, but I couldn't, so I tried to think of other people I could show the cake to. Mrs. Rayburn would be happy that I had made a presentable dessert. Aeslynn would probably laugh. Every time I did a new stitch correctly I showed it to her with pride and she'd laugh, saying, "I've never met a lass with more pride in her accomplishments. Well done, Edith." Edith, the unknown woman who led me to a boarding-house kitchen in Philadelphia. What would she think of a frosted cake?

I realized the Edith I had created in Chicago wasn't a woman who would pack one outfit and fourteen gifts in her well-aged suitcase. I figured her age was reflected in the wrinkles in its leather. As I saw her in Philadelphia, Edith Shay was an older woman who had seen the events I considered history unfold.

Perhaps she was a woman like Mrs. Rayburn, who would sit down beside me and tell the stories of her past with kindness and a sense of instruction. She would tell me the proper way to scrub a floor and cook a meal. We could sit out on the porch on sunny afternoons and take in God's beauty. Grandma Margaret always said the silence of nature is the best speech a person can hear. If you listen carefully, you forget yourself and you start to see how full the world really is, right down to the tiny ants that crawl on your shoes.

Edith would rock, making the floor boards on her verandah squeak. A breeze would blow and make her think of a story to tell. "I was no cotillion maid, if you catch my meaning." She'd lean toward me, a smile slowly spreading across her face. "No sir, I was off watching the birds or collecting wildflowers. Never saw the use of sitting pretty when you could have your hands elbow-deep in life."

"Edith!" Mrs. Rayburn's exclamation brought me back to the boarding-house kitchen in Philadelphia. I was sitting in front of a frosted cake with the knife I had used sinking into the top. The stew was boiling over, and the table hadn't been set.

"Sorry, Mrs. Rayburn." I jumped off the stool and ran to take the pot off the stove.

The dining room filled with conversation as the meal began. Two gallons of beef stew disappeared, and Mr. Shultz had two slices of my cake. He was so pleased with it that he didn't even notice he had stained his cuff with frosting when he cut his second piece. Mrs. Rayburn took him aside when he left the table and offered to clean the suit coat. He blushed, but she was scrubbing it in the kitchen sink when I came in the next morning.

"My stars, I plain forgot." She dropped the suit into the dry sink, then walked to the corner of the kitchen where my satchel sat on the floor. "Vivian brought this over last night after you went to bed."

"Thank you. It'll be nice to wear something familiar again." Mrs. Rayburn lifted her brows in surprise. "I'm sorry, Mrs. Rayburn. I loved the dress you gave me. I just miss what's familiar, what smells like home."

"I saw how you loved my dress. It took me close to two hours to scrub out all that ink."

"I'm so sorry about that. I wasn't using my head."

"It looked more like you were using your knees." She smiled. "Now get off to work before Mr. Denison decides to fire you."

"Yes, ma'am."

I finished scrubbing the floor by nine and set to work on the letter boxes before Mr. Denison said a word. He came out of his office at a quarter to ten and searched the floor as if he expected to find me there. When he noticed me sitting at the table below the window, I froze, afraid that he'd object. He shifted his weight from one foot to the other, then walked to the front door and opened for business. That day, I boxed books— fighting the urge to pick one up and read it— cleaned up ink spills, and washed the windows. Each time Mr. Denison gave me a new task, I asked "Excuse me sir, but exactly how do you want this done?"

Every set of instructions started the same way.

"Any fool knows how this is done." He often added, "I swear you were raised in a foreign country, girl."

Philadelphia did seem like it was in a separate country from Wisconsin. With a park large enough to get lost in for days, it had trees and grass galore, but there were cobblestone streets, buildings bigger than barns with fancy facades that made them look more like sculptures than buildings. And the buildings were older than the country itself, with some places dating back to the sixteen-hundreds. The ancient city seemed set apart even from Chicago. The shipyard wasn't just a kingdom of commerce. They built new ships there; ships with steel hulls that resisted the rotting strength of the water. Mrs. Rayburn told me the East Coast was a miniature world unto itself. A person could travel through five states or more in a day's time if they were on a train traveling along the ocean.

The Atlantic Ocean was only a few hours away by train. An ocean was too big to fit into my thoughts. It took months to travel across; it was filled with creatures larger than the enormous ships that hoisted over a hundred sails. And I had also heard about the Pacific Ocean far across the frontier on the other side of the

Mexican territories. The fish there were so fantastic, they could fly.

I wanted to work my way out West. My husband and I would face the desert no-man's-land—cross it in a rumbling stagecoach—ride over the mountains to a land where oranges grew in groves. If we went far enough, we could watch the waves of the Pacific Ocean crashing against the rocks. My ocean fantasy carried me through another day under Mr. Denison.

On the way to the boarding house, I worked through the figures to see how long I would have to endure Mr. Denison. According to my sums, I would have to work there for only ten days. This made me happy enough to try making custard for dinner. It was a success, along with the corn fritters and the honey-cured ham Mrs. Rayburn had brought home from the butcher shop. The plates were clean enough to be washed without a rag after the guests were through with their meals.

After I cleaned the kitchen, Mrs. Rayburn and I spent the evening in the parlor. It was usually empty after dark, because the guests spent their time either in their rooms or joining the conversation that was bound to be going on in the mercantile across the street. Mrs. Rayburn was knitting as I paged through the newspaper. The *Philadelphia Public Ledger* was a hundred years older than the *Chicago Tribune,* and the printing presses that made it must have been older than Mr. Denison's. Half the consonants were chipped or blurred. Flaws aside, it was still nice to work my way through a paper, but the words didn't draw me in. I wasn't interested in reading anything. My mind couldn't hold onto a thought long enough for me to read an entire article. I was too tired, I suppose. I liked the familiar look of the boxed advertisements with their elaborate sketches, the tight columns, and the bold headlines designed to fishhook the reader's eye and reel him in to read the articles. Taking it all in made me feel at home. I could imagine the rough pine walls in my mind and hear the rhythmic squeals of Grandpa Jacob's chair as he rocked.

"Never known a girl to read the paper. I buy it for my guests to read. A young man brings it to the door. I'm sure the delivery boy changes from year to year, but they all look the same to me, freckles and a red cap. They all have freckles and a red cap."

"I've always loved reading papers. There's so much inside them."

"You find livelihood or a roof for over your head in there?"

"They have employment and rental information."

"How about a husband? You find a man looking for a sweetheart in there?"

"No, I haven't."

"Well, don't let these jobs fool you, Edith. You can't live like this forever. You need a man who can take care of you, or you'll be walking from one job to the next all your life. There's no room for a family in that."

So true. I'd never build a home if I was moving from job to job. I'd see the world, but who would see it with me? I couldn't see myself in a small house washing clothes, cooking corn muffins, and chasing kids away from the pie safe, but it hurt to think of being alone. I didn't want to be a stranger all of my life—having to learn the rules of a new boss, deciding what and what not to say about myself.

"Edith?" Mrs. Rayburn pressed me to speak, but I had too many questions even to respond. Where would I stop? When? At what point could I really say, "I've seen enough of the world, I'll live right here"? I didn't know the answers. I only knew enough to say Philadelphia wasn't my home.

"Edith?"

"Sorry, you certainly gave me something to

think about." I folded the paper in my lap. Forcing a laugh, I said, "And what man would want to start a family with a bumble foot like me?"

"Don't you listen to Lawford Denison. He hides his own flaws by exaggerating the flaws of others. You're a bright, beautiful girl. You'll make a fine wife someday."

"Perhaps, but not today. I have to save up for the delivery I'm making to Virginia."

She smiled and nodded. I added, "I figured it out today. I should make enough for a ticket to Washington by the end of next week or the beginning of the next."

"Hmm." Mrs. Rayburn hummed as she went back to her knitting. After a moment of silence, she said, "Don't take this as disrespect for a fellow citizen, but I wouldn't count on leaving here too soon."

"What do you mean?"

"Mr. Denison doesn't do enough daily business to pay his employees on a weekly basis. You'll be lucky if he pays you at the end of the month."

"He never said a word about that."

"He didn't have to, you were desperate."

Mrs. Rayburn's warning pushed me into Mr. Denison's office that Friday. I stood by the doorway waiting for him to look up from his

proofreading and acknowledge I was there. He
didn't. I whispered, "Excuse me."

"Yes, what is it?"

"I was wondering sir, when will I be paid?"

He dropped his fountain pen, then glared at
me. "You are an unending bundle of iniquities,
aren't you?"

"Pardon me?"

"Failures! An endless bundle of failures. You're
uneducated, disobedient, clumsy, and greedy.
You come begging at my doorstep with nothing
to offer but an old, broken suitcase filled with
trinkets and clothes."

I was instantly mad enough to break glass
with a bare fist. He had rifled through Edith's
things. How dare he? I wanted to rant and rave
until his ears fell off, but I wasn't going to give
him any reason to withhold my wages, so I
calmly said, "I don't see how this is any of your
concern, Mr. Denison. I simply want to know
when I'll be paid, so I can plan my departure for
Washington."

"You'll be paid at the end of the month."

The end of the month arrived with freezing
winds. As the clock struck one that afternoon,
I watched as each typesetter entered the office
in turn. They emerged from the office with a
white envelope in their vest pocket. I assumed

this was the routine for receiving wages, so I entered Mr. Denison's office after the last type-setter left.

"Yes, Miss Shay?"

"May I receive my wages, please?"

Mr. Denison replied without looking up from the ledger book he was examining. "I'm afraid we've run short this month, Miss Shay. You'll have to wait for the end of next month."

"But, but you said I would be paid at the end of this month. I've been planning to leave for Richmond for weeks."

"I don't see where you're in any position to tell me what I can and cannot do, Miss Shay. Now either wait for your wages or leave without them."

I left the office in tears. Vivian caught me by the elbow and led me to the back room. "Miss Shay, my husband is a stern man, but I swear to you on God's good name that he's an honest one. We sincerely do not have the money to pay you at this time. Might I remind you, we took you in out of charity. The least you can do in return is show patience."

"Patience!" Mrs. Rayburn scowled in her chair by the fireplace in the parlor. I had told her everything, and her response was unexpected.

"I shouldn't be surprised that Vivian would use such a word, she's been telling herself the same lie for years."

"How so?"

"She's been trying to have a child for nearly twenty years. Every time she loses a child she blames it on her impatience. She believes the Lord will give her a child if she is patient enough. She uses the example of Sarah to keep her hopes alive. It's got nothing to do with patience. Either the Lord wishes for you to be with child or He doesn't. And that husband of hers would steal from Christ himself if he thought he could get away with it. But don't you worry, you'll get what's rightfully yours. I'll see to that." She said it as if it was a fact she'd read in the daily paper, and started knitting.

Sitting there in silence, I began to think of Aeslynn. She'd hired me on the spot—not out of charity, but because she believed I could learn something from her. I received my pay in a crisp white envelope every Friday evening. Aeslynn never scolded me as Elly did. I don't think Aeslynn had a cruel bone in her body. She was a true saint next to the demanding beast of a man—that rude old Lawford Denison. I owed her so much.

She deserved more than a silent good-bye on

a train platform. At the least, I owed her the truth. I had to write her a letter. I didn't have the money to buy paper, so I had to ask Mrs. Rayburn for something to write on.

"Oh child." She shook her head as she dropped her knitting into the basket by her chair. "If I had only known. Your parents must be feverish with worry by this time." I followed her back to a small room facing the hospital. The furniture had an untouched look about it. The lace table-cloth under the lamp by the window was perfectly straight. The pipes on the humidor were lined up as if they were on display in a store window. In fact, the whole room reminded me of the displays I used to set up in Mrs. Bowfield's window. Better yet, they looked like the ones in the department store windows in Chicago—the beautiful rolltop desk complete with inkwell, blotter, and carefully sorted letters.

"This was Mason's study. He used to write to doctors all over the world. He was always searching for new ways to treat his patients."

I had such an urge to read the letters poking out of the cubbyholes in the desk. They probably came from all over Europe: England, Germany, Norway—perhaps there were even letters from as far away as China. I had always heard the Chinese had medical secrets that were centuries old, or so Grandpa Jacob said. He heard all kinds of stories about the Chinese from his old friends who still worked for the railroad.

Mrs. Rayburn opened a wooden box on the desktop and drew out a handful of paper and envelopes. "Take it all, and I don't want to hear another word about it. I'm not much for letter writing, and Mason would want his paper used."

"Thank you." I accepted the gift with a smile, but I really wanted to hug her for her kindness. I turned about and was heading for my room when Mrs. Rayburn yelled, "Do you need an inkwell and a quill?"

"I have a pencil, thank you!" I shouted from the stairs. My pencil was short, but it worked just fine. I sat down and used the trunk at the end of the bed as a desk to write.

Dear Aeslynn,
    I must confess that my wild heart has got-
ten me into some trouble. Don't fret, I'm just
fine.

No, that wasn't right. I would worry her needlessly, and knowing Aeslynn she'd send me money. I was hiding from what I really had to tell her.

Aeslynn,

I have a confession to make. I haven't been quite truthful with you. When I look back on that day we met in your shop, I can't quite recall what made me do it, perhaps I was too nervous to correct you, or maybe I liked the idea of leaving my old self behind and beginning anew in Chicago. In any case, I should have stopped you when you called me "Edith."

You see, the suitcase I carry isn't my own. I found it abandoned or perhaps misplaced in a Michigan train station. In fact, I'm on a journey to return it. I've simply made a stop in Pennsylvania to

I wanted to tell her I was doing it to avoid traveling in snowstorms or to enjoy the New Year in an old-fashioned city, but I couldn't tell a lie while I was trying to confess to another, so I wrote

raise enough money to reach Richmond, Virginia. That's where the real Edith Shay is from. As for me, the real me, I am from a place in Wisconsin that the locals call "Lunden Woods." They call it that because my family's lived there since the trapping days before the Revolution. My name is truly Katherine. Katherine Candace Lunden. I wanted you to know, because you've given me so much and I gave you a lie in return. You deserve to know the truth. All of it. I left Wisconsin without my parents' permission. That's why they were so angry with me. I've written to tell them how I feel about traveling, but I don't know their response. I have no right to ask more of you, Aeslynn, but could you check with Mr. Quince to see if I received a letter from them? You can forward it here to Philadelphia. I'll be here until the end of the month.

Please forgive me for this terrible lie and know that I owe you my life as it is now. You gave me the courage to keep going.

With great appreciation,
Katherine Lunden

The next morning, I walked to the post office before work. As I traveled, I noticed that the ice hanging from the eaves on the buildings was beginning to melt. The dirty snow piled along the edges of the streets was spotted with water-filled footprints. It wouldn't be long before the birds started coming back, I thought as I stepped into the post office. I sent the letter off with a prayer that Aeslynn would forgive me. I also hoped she could send my parents' letter off in enough time so that it reached me before I left for Richmond. Then again, who was to say my parents had even sent a letter? There was nothing I could do but pray and wait.

I waited through twenty-eight days—trudging through the same routine on weekdays—thanking God on each morning that February was a short month. Walking through the slush and muck on the streets, I arrived at eight A.M. to scrub the floor. Then I spent three hours at the table by the window, cleaning type, because Mr. Denison didn't want any ink to build up on his priceless letters. I was beginning to lose sight of the difference between soaking them on an occasional basis and rubbing them clean every day. I washed the windows every Thursday and cleaned and polished the machines on Friday afternoons.

The only interruption to my weekly schedule was a three-day period in the middle of the month when one of the typesetters fell ill. Mr. Denison shoved me into his position. On the first day, he stood at my side to monitor my work. There was a handwritten manuscript pinned to the wall in front of me and I had to copy it letter for letter by filling a printed sled called a chase with the tiny little letters I usually cleaned. The only handwriting I'd ever read had been my family's. That was no preparation for the stringy mess on the pages I was supposed to copy. It reminded me of the thread left on the bottom of a sewing box, all knotted and jumbled. I often misread the writing and placed the wrong letter in the sled. Mr. Denison cracked me over the knuckles with a ruler every time I made a mistake.

"That's an *r* not an *h,*" he'd scream, and slam the ruler down. My shoulders stiffened, because I was hunched forward to read, then I jolted into an upright position every time I saw the ruler raised out of the corner of my eye. My fingers began to throb, and I found myself checking the clock at five-minute intervals.

Mr. Denison didn't give me a moment's rest until he started to sway, putting all his weight on one foot, then the other. He was getting tired. Around three P.M., he put the ruler on the counter next to me, then turned to the closest typesetter. "Franklin, check all her work!"

I had never been introduced to any of the typesetters. Suddenly knowing one of their names made it necessary to know more. "Have you worked here long?" I asked when I was sure Mr. Denison had returned to his office. Franklin didn't even turn his head.

"No talking!" Mr. Denison yelled.

No was the key word of my existence for an entire month. No, you cannot have your wages.

No, you cannot leave early to attend a tea social at Mrs. Rayburn's. No, you didn't clean this floor well enough, do it again. Mr. Denison had me so twisted up I didn't know what I could and couldn't do anymore.

Back home I'd rolled up my sleeves and chipped my way through pine tar and soot to clean out Mother's stove so it was as good as the day it came from Mankato. I'd learned to split a log into shingles after the chicken coop was struck by a tree. I could sew a ballgown with my own two hands if I had to. I could even cook a five-course meal for a party of fourteen, but Mr. Denison had me thinking I couldn't even lace my own boots. I was shrinking in that old print shop, disappearing. I felt so low about myself, my birthday passed and I didn't even know it until Mrs. Rayburn asked me to put a candle in the supper cake for Mr. Shultz on the twenty-fifth of February. I'd turned seventeen on the seventeenth and hadn't even remembered it was my birthday. I put a candle in Mr. Shultz's cake and laughed.

I felt a bit like crying. Missing my own birthday was like forgetting myself. I wondered what else I'd lost or forgotten, but then Mrs. Rayburn called for the cake from the dining room. I put it out of my mind for a while, setting the cake in the middle of the table with the candle burning, imagining that the people at that table were really members of my family.

That night, I realized there were only three days left before I could leave, but there was still no letter from Aeslynn or my parents. I had already promised to deliver Mrs. Rayburn's presents. I couldn't disappoint her. I had to leave for Washington city. The only solution was to ask Mrs. Rayburn to send the letters on to me when I found the real Edith Shay. But that brought me face to face with my lie again. What excuse could I use with Mrs. Rayburn? That I was so used to the name that I forgot it wasn't my own? She would think me mad. I had to tell her, but she'd never trust her presents to a liar. I decided to tell her as I'd told Aeslynn, after the fact, when it could no longer hurt me. For those last three days, I felt a chill in my heart every time Mrs. Rayburn called me Edith, but I knew I'd only hurt her more by telling the truth before her presents were safely in her grandchildren's hands.

On the twenty-eighth, I entered Mr. Denison's office after Franklin left with his wage envelope. There was a white envelope on the edge of his desk. The name *Edith Shay* was written on it in tall, straight letters that were so precise they could have been printed with the letters I spent so much time cleaning. I stepped forward half-expecting Mr. Denison to grab the envelope at the last minute. When it was safely in my hand, I backed away from the desk to say, "Thank you, Mr. Denison. I'm quite grateful."

"As you should be," Denison spoke more to the papers he was reading than me.

I was about to ask him for my suitcase when Mrs. Denison, who sat at the small desk along the wall, cleared her throat.

"Enough!" Mr. Denison stood up. "Miss Shay, I have decided that a letter of recommendation is in order. So, here it is." The stiff, intense way with which he avoided looking at his wife told me the letter was her idea.

"A letter of recommendation?" I asked as he handed me a second envelope. "For another boarding house?"

"No, you fool!" He turned to his wife. "I told you she didn't have the sense to call two nickels a dime!"

Mrs. Denison rose, then came to stand next to me. Cupping my elbows, she said, "Miss Shay, all in all, you've done good work for us here. We wanted to help you get gainful employment in the place you wish to settle."

"Really?"

"Certainly. Simply present this letter of recommendation when you apply for a job."

"Thank you," I whispered.

The letter I held could speak for my skills, and
I wouldn't have to enter another hotel from the
back door as long as I lived. I felt like kissing Mrs.
Denison on the cheek, but she probably would
have fainted from embarrassment. I was so excited
I almost ran to tell Doreen before I got my suitcase.

Turning I said, "Mr. Denison?"

"What is it now?"

"May I have my suitcase back?"

"What?"

"My suitcase, can I have it? I will be leaving
soon."

"In two weeks."

The thought of it made me whine. "Two
weeks?"

"That's right. Our agreement was that you
would give a two weeks' resignation notice. I
will consider this your resignation. Your position will be terminated in two week's time. You
will have to retrieve your wages in person at the
end of the month."

As I saw it, Denison was exacting his revenge
for being forced to write the letter of recommendation. His cruelty stunned me. I wandered
out of the office in a daze. In the street, my anger

bubbled up inside me. Holding up the letter, I had half a mind to tear it up and throw the pieces in that man's face like so much corn, but I wouldn't let him pull me into acting like a fool. His letter would open doors for me, and I wasn't about to destroy the one good thing I got out of working for Lawford Denison.

Walking back to Doreen's, I thought about opening the letter. If I did, the next employer would know I had. Denison had sealed it with wax that bore his mark. Then again, he could have said awful things about me that would paint me as the town fool in front of a prospective employer. Denison was certainly cruel enough to derive some pleasure from knowing I would be standing in front of an employer expecting a look of respect and receiving an order to leave by the back door.

Sitting on the steps of a townhouse, I opened the letter. I'd replace the envelope and seal it with wax. It was unlikely anyone would recognize Lawford's seal anyhow. The letter read:

February 28th, 1870

To Whom It May Concern,
    I, Lawford Denison, the proprietor of the Denison Printing Press of Philadelphia, do solemnly swear that Miss Edith Shay has the

skill and commitment to complete the work appropriate to a printer's apprentice. In my service, she has cleaned and set type as well as observed the daily routine of a printing press with interest and intelligence. In my opinion, she would make a fine apprentice if one were to overlook her limitations as a member of the frailer sex and her better suitability for cleaning and general housekeeping.

Sincerely,
Lawford Denison

His reference to me as a printer's apprentice chilled my veins with pride, but I was ready to throw rocks by the time I reached his line about the "frailer sex" and housekeeping. I'd like to see him mop up an inky floor any faster than I could. In fact, I pictured him doing just that— on his hands and knees—soaking up all the ink in his fine suit. I might not be strong enough to shovel coal or fell a tree, but I could cook, clean, and print circles around that puny tyrant. His only power was fear. He used yelling to inflate his own strength. If anything, he was the weakling, hiding behind all his insults and shouts and threats.

Standing up, I turned to go back to his shop. Tucking the letter into my pocket with the firm promise to myself that I wouldn't let him have it back, I marched straight into his office. "Mr. Denison." I spoke firmly, but I didn't raise my voice. Only the devil needs to shout, my mother used to say.

"What now?"

"You have no right to hold my suitcase. I told you of my intention of leaving last month. As I see it, I've given you a month's notice."

He stared at me like I'd just slapped him in the face. His lips sputtered. He gripped the edge of his desk as if he was going to snap it off.

"How dare you!" He breathed the words out like an ancient curse.

"I dare because although you've given me a job for the sake of Christian charity, you've done nothing but treat me poorly since the moment I began work. I am not a child, Mr. Denison. I am a young woman who has proven herself worthy of your respect. But to be truthful, I don't want it. I want my suitcase."

He sprang from his desk and charged at the wardrobe behind it as if he were attacking a wild animal. Flinging the door open, he yanked out my suitcase and sent it flying across the floor. "Take the piece of junk." Marching forward, he pointed at me, shouting, "And if you ever so much as show your face in this shop again, I'll have you arrested for trespassing."

Picking up the suitcase, I nodded, saying, "Thank you."

In the street, I let out a shout of triumph. He was just a scared little man after all—just spits and spouts of yelling. That's all there was to him. I practically ran home to tell Doreen. She'd started supper on my behalf, but I'd done what I had to do.

And when I began to tell her my story, she stepped away from the stove, wiping her hands on the towel over her shoulder, then sat down on the stool to listen. As I finished, she clapped her hands, saying, "Bravo, child. That man deserves a good stripping of the soul. He's got so much greed and anger hanging off him, he wouldn't fit through the gates of heaven."

I couldn't keep myself from laughing, and she joined me. I shook my head in disbelief. I'd really stood up to Mr. Denison. My heart felt so light, I bet I could have flown to Washington.

Gifts

Despite my triumph over Denison, I woke up with a heavy heart on March the first. I realized I had been building walls behind me as I traveled. My parents were so hurt over my leaving home that they told me I could never come back. And how could I face Aeslynn after lying to her? I was about to build yet another wall, between myself and Mrs. Rayburn, by leaving Philadelphia without telling her who I really was.

I had to tell her the truth, but what would she think of me then? Would she trust me with the gifts? I needed time to think. Mixing the pancake batter was oddly soothing that morning. It gave me time to sort out my thoughts.

A. LaFaye

"Were you hoping it'll turn into rock?" Mrs. Rayburn's voice startled me.

"What?"

"You keep stirring that batter and you'll be able to iron with those griddle cakes."

"Oh." I blushed.

"I thought you'd be excited about moving on."

I turned to face her, wiping my hands on my apron. "You know, I could use a little time to rest. I've been working these two jobs and worrying about what Mr. Denison will do. I feel all worn out." It made no sense to lie so that I would have time to admit to another lie, but I couldn't stop myself.

"You do look a little like an old sheet that's been out on the line too long." Mrs. Rayburn took the bowl from me and walked to the stove. "If you don't mind keeping up with your work around here for a day or two, I would appreciate the time to find a replacement."

"All right." The idea that I was helping Mrs. Rayburn made me feel lighter, almost happy. Maybe telling her the truth wouldn't be so hard after all, I thought.

Sitting in the parlor that evening, I was prepared to confess. Each time I looked up to begin, she'd stop her knitting, then say, "Yes, Edith?"

Hearing that name stopped me. Then I had to make up some new fabrication to explain why I'd interrupted her work. I asked her all kinds of out-of-the-way questions like, "Have you advertised for the position?" or "How does your son like living in the capital?"

She gladly answered each one, happy to talk. A sign in the window of a local cafe and one in the front window of her house worked just fine for drawing in new cooks, and her son was thrilled to be in Washington.

"And they have the finest schools for my grandchildren," Mrs. Rayburn added as she examined her own handiwork.

I nodded and smiled to feign interest, but I was really boiling in my own guilt. If felt as if I were burning from the inside out. I had to tell her, but I couldn't destroy her confidence in me.

That night, as I got into bed, I thought about the note I'd leave. I'd wait for her to find a replacement, then slip it into her knitting basket as I left for the train station. That way she would know the truth, but my deceit wouldn't keep her from trusting me with the gifts for her grandchildren. Delivering them would be the least I could do to repay her.

I got out of bed to write the note, for fear that I'd lose the nerve to do so by morning.

Dear Mrs. Rayburn,

I cannot begin to explain my reasons, but trust me when I say that I truly hope you can forgive me for the lie I've told you. My name is really Katherine Lunden. I've taken the name Edith Shay as a matter of confused circumstances. I'm running from no one, and I've come by the name through an honest mistake, not any act of treachery. I tell you this now to ask you for one last favor. A letter may come for me in the near future.

I was panicked. What could I tell her? Where could she send it? I heard Mrs. Rayburn in the dining room telling Mr. Shultz to eat the eggs she'd cooked. Then it came to me.

Please send it to Katherine Lunden, care of Edith Shay, 1919 Fillmore Lane, Richmond, Virginia.

I'm truly grateful for all you've done for me. Please forgive me for my lack of honesty and know that I value your friendship.

With gratitude,
Katherine Lunden

I tucked the letter into my coat pocket so I wouldn't forget to leave it for her.

• • •

As the days passed, I felt quite good. I wasn't forever fretting over money or travel plans or carefully kept lies. For the first time in months, I was free to live my life an hour at a time. I even took the time to visit the library and read a book for the sure pleasure of it. Called *Mary Washington Abroad,* it was a fanciful story about a girl traveling to Europe aboard a ship with her chaperon and enough luggage to break the wheels on a stagecoach. After reading about all the little rules Mary's stuffy chaperon, Mrs. Havishel, insisted upon—don't look men in the eye, never speak of money in public, gloves are to be worn out of doors at all times—I was almost glad I was traveling alone. All the rules poor Mary had to follow would have driven me to flee straight home.

Home. I certainly missed. it. On the way back to Mrs. Rayburn's, I thought of the picnic we had every summer on the hill behind the church. Always the third Sunday in June, rain or shine, it was our celebration of summer. Everyone in town was there, the women wearing new dresses, the men sporting store-bought shirts and maybe even a new hat. The kids had already broken in their new pants with all their running and fishing and tadpole hunting. I loved the games. We had barrel-rim races. You had to use a stick to push your rim along. Thomas could even run with two wheels spinning. I often tripped over mine, but it was the fun of it that counted. Grandpa Jacob was the reigning watermelon-seed spitting champion. My mother had won the best pie contest three years running with her cherry rhubarb pie. You couldn't even tell she used preserved fruit. I could taste that sweet-tart pie as I stepped in the back door.

"That you, Edith?" Mrs. Rayburn called from the parlor.

"Yes, ma'am."

"You got a letter in the post today. I put it on your bed."

I was halfway up the stairs before she was through speaking. My hands were shaking like the lid on a boiling pot when I picked up the envelope. It was thick and from Aeslynn. I ripped it open praying there was something from Mother and Father inside. Aeslynn had wrapped her letter around two others. I read it in a rush. She said:

February 27, 1870

Kait,

Do you mind if I call you "Kait," lass? All Katherines are Kaits where I come from. Anyhow, can't say as I was too surprised by your letter. You were a secret keeper from the beginning. By the way, Mrs. Hessmueller says she was amazed you could sew a stitch after the way you handled yourself in the Greymore's kitchen. We're doing their sheets now, and I told Elly to sew a little soot into the seams so they'll turn black in the wash. Crabby old Mrs. Hessmueller might blame it on the maids, but they're probably used to her ranting and raving by now.

What did hurt me though, was thinking how you were waiting to hear from your ma and your da, praying they'd forgive you. They will my darling, and I'm almost sure these letters I send on to you say just that. Can you believe, I left the post office reading your letter as I went. I was in the middle of the street when I got to the part about waiting for a letter from your parents, so I marched right back. And the saints be praised, Mr. Quince was holding two letters for you. He said he'd been holding the one since early January.

I'm praying they reach you, even though I just got them today. I told God to put on your brakes so you don't leave Philadelphia before these letters arrive. But if you do go first, and I half-believe you will, I know God will get these letters to you in His own time.

> *I miss you, lass. Enough to say, you better write and write often or I'll haunt you when I die.*
>
> > *With much affection,*
> > *Aeslynn O'Dell*

I was laughing through tears as I folded her letter. Aeslynn O'Dell was a fine woman. If only my own mother would be so understanding, I thought as I opened the next letter. It was dated the nineteenth of December. My heart skipped a beat to think that my family had been missing me as much as I'd missed them that Christmas. I was sobbing before I finished the first line. It took me a while to finish the letter with all of my tears.

> *Dearest Katherine,*
>
> *Today we decorated the Christmas tree. Father and Thomas hiked out past the Huddleston farm to find just the right one. It was full enough to touch both walls when we put it in the corner by the back door.*
>
> *I was willing to accept your absence until I took your ornament out of the trimmings box. You remember it, don't you dear? That silver angel your grandfather had engraved with your name in LaCrosse. I'm not ashamed to say I sat down right there and cried.*

*Katherine, this is your home. You belong
here with your family. Come home. Celebrate
Christmas with us. Your angel is waiting on
top of the mantel. I'll have no one but you
hang it on the tree.*

    Love,
        Mother and Father

      Love you,
        Riney, Thomas

        Miss you,
          Grandma and Grandpa

I wanted to run to the train station, buy a ticket
home, and telegraph Mother when I reached
Michigan, but I didn't move. Something held me
there, sitting on the bed, the letters resting in my
lap. To go back seemed wrong somehow. But
how could it? My parents wanted me back home.
I missed them so much I ached. The answer was
there, but I couldn't hear it.

I picked up the last letter, hoping I'd know
why I felt so divided.

              February 17, 1870

Katherine,
   *It was raining the day you were born. It's
never rained in February over the seventeen*

years since then. Grandpa Jacob said God was getting the world clean just for you to see. Grandma Margaret gave you your first bath in rainwater. Rain was your birthright. You'd go a mile out of your way to play in a puddle when you were a child.

But by the time you were working for Mrs. Bowfield, you hated rain. It made you sad. I suppose that was the first warning you'd be walking away from the place you were born to. Part of me knew then, but I wasn't ready to listen. I still thought I could keep you home.

Happy birthday Katherine, may all your dreams come true.

Love,
Mother

My mother knew me well after all. She couldn't bring herself to say it, but in that final line, she'd given me what I wanted, her blessing to pursue my own dreams. I felt so loved. So accepted. Mother had finally seen me for who I was—a girl with her heart hitched to a star, as Grandpa Jacob used to say. I had to keep going. And my mother was pushing me forward.

I sat down and wrote to my family.

March 5, 1870

Hello everyone,

My heart feels like it just woke up after a long bout with a fever. I'm so glad to hear you have welcomed me back into your home. And I will be there when I can be. I've got something I must do first. Someone I must meet. I intend to explain it all to you when I get home. I'll be there soon, I promise.

Until then, know that I love you and I miss you. I promise to keep in touch.

All my love,
Katherine

When the letter was finished, I took it straight to the post office. As I stood in line, I thought of Aeslynn. Racing back to Mrs. Rayburn's, I dashed off a little note.

Aeslynn,

You are truly a treasure. Thank you for understanding. I received your package. I'm sending off a letter today, so my parents will know I'm well in no time at all. Thank you so much, Aeslynn. I'll write often. Too often, you'll say when you look back in a year's time.

With admiration,
Kait

Once the letters were in the post, all that was left to be done was find a replacement for me in Mrs. Rayburn's kitchen. The first candidate put salt instead of sugar in her cake batter and served half-raw roast beef without any vegetables. Mrs. Rayburn sent the second young lady out the back door before she even finished cooking the meal. The foolish girl had put too much wood in the stove and nearly burned her hair off when she lifted a burner plate.

My replacement arrived on March the seventh in a wool dress the color of a well-cooked pumpkin pie. She carried a black leather satchel and umbrella and didn't even wait for Mrs. Rayburn's ground rules. Hanging her coat by the back door and setting her satchel by the stairs, she set to work, saying, "I don't work on the Lord's day, but I can cook anything you care to request. I rise by five A.M. and have the kitchen clean for the night by seven. I expect to have my evenings and Saturday afternoons free and to have fresh linens in my room once a week."

I knew she was hired without waiting to hear Mrs. Rayburn's response. I was in what used to be my room, when Mrs. Rayburn came to say, "I expect you'll be on your way to the train station then?"

"Yes, ma'am."

"I'll take you after I get Miss Newton settled."

"Good." I stepped into the hall, Edith's suitcase in hand. "I'll meet you on the porch."

I slipped my note into Mrs. Rayburn's knitting basket as I went outside. Mrs. Rayburn came only a few minutes later. "I'd better watch that woman. She'll be running the place if I don't."

"Probably so." I smiled.

We locked arms as we stepped into the street to make our way to the station. I said a short prayer that she'd forgive me, as we walked. While we waited in the ticket line, she checked the packages to make sure they were sealed. We waited on a bench in the lobby for the train to arrive.

"You take good care of these things." She patted the packages sitting between us. "I put a lot of love into buying these gifts. I want them to be fresh and new when the children open them."

I nodded, and she turned to face the clock. "The train arrives in an hour. You'll board and be there before noon tomorrow. I suggest you go straight to the house. The children won't be home from school yet. It'll give their mother time to get over the surprise of a stranger bearing gifts."

"Are you sure you don't want to come with me? They'd be awful glad to see you."

"Yes, well, I can't close up my doors and expect

customers to be there when I return." She checked the tightness of the string on the packages. "Besides, it's a son's duty to visit his mother, not the other way around."

When the boarding call came, she jumped up from her seat. She couldn't keep her hands still. They darted back and forth from the packages to me. She straightened my collar, then dusted the boxes, buttoned my coat, then tested the string. "You have the letter now?"

"Yes, ma'am."

"Your ticket?"

"Yes."

"Dear." She touched her lips. "I'm acting like your grandmother, aren't I?"

"A little." I smiled. "You haven't spit-cleaned the spots on my face yet."

"Heavens." She blushed.

"They'll love your gifts, Mrs. Rayburn." I kissed her on the cheek and she smiled. "I'm sure they'll be out to see you real soon."

"Of course." She stiffened.

I picked up the packages and my suitcase and we walked out to the platform. I boarded the train, and she froze in place. There was no reason for it. For a fleeting moment, I thought she'd turned to stone. Perhaps she was so full of emotions she didn't know which one to show.

Mrs. Rayburn didn't wave from the platform. She watched silently as I boarded the train with the suitcase in one hand and her packages under the other arm. Her eyes followed me as I backed away, but her lips never moved. I waved from my seat. She didn't even twitch. The train pulled away from the station and she was still standing in the exact same position.

As the train pulled out of the station, I kept hearing Mrs. Rayburn saying, "You can't live like this forever. . . . There's no room for a family."

It made me feel so empty inside. I could dream all I wanted about Edith Shay, but no matter who she was, she wasn't my family. She would never be my mother or an Aeslynn O'Dell or a Doreen Rayburn. She'd be someone new, someone completely different whom I'd have to get to know.

I was in a daze, pondering just what the real Edith Shay would be like, when the conductor came through to collect tickets. The silver buttons on his coat glinted in the light of the lanterns and made me think of Buford's long watch fob that used to sway when he walked. Thinking of Buford made me long for a good paper.

As the conductor asked for my ticket, I said, "You wouldn't happen to have a newspaper, would you?"

"Yes ma'am, I do. But I must say that I value my reading material highly. If I lent it to you, I'd expect to receive it back in mint condition."

"Certainly." I felt a swirl of excitement in my chest. I should have been ashamed of myself, a near-grown woman, getting all giddy over a newspaper. You'd think I'd written the entire thing myself.

He brought the paper back and I dove right in. A rambunctious child had thrown a rock through a window at Independence Hall. The plans for the Fourth of July celebrations for the city of Philadelphia were already underway, and a local munitions factory was putting its war talents to good use by producing the fireworks. They promised a display that would turn the Philadelphia night sky into day. All the stories of the city made me realize I'd never really been there. I'd debarked in their train station, walked down their streets, lived in a boarding house, and worked in a print shop, but I had barely visited the library let alone all the monuments of our country—Independence Hall, the Liberty Bell, the homes of all the men who shaped our country. I'd been so bent on my destination, I forgot to enjoy the journey. What a fool. I promised myself that once I finished the little favor for Mrs. Rayburn, I would slow my pace down and take in the country I was passing through.

That little favor turned into a lot more. I had to disembark in the Washington station and find my way to Mrs. Rayburn's son's house. I approached a ticket clerk for directions. "Excuse me, where is 716 D Street Northeast?"

"How do you plan to get there?"

"On foot."

He blinked as if he was trying to get a thought to come to mind. "Young lady, that's got to be three miles from here at the very least. You'd better hire a coach."

"A coach?"

"A cab."

"Oh, I know what you meant, I just don't think I have the money for it."

"Suit yourself."

"How much is a ticket to Virginia?"

"I haven't any idea. We don't have a line going down there. The Confederate rail companies have their offices in Arlington. They're too stubborn to reopen their Washington offices."

"Arlington!"

"Young lady, do you have anyone else with you?"

"No." He was bordering on an insult, so I turned to leave before I did something rash. "Thank you."

A. LaFaye

He blinked again without response.

The coach fare was seventy-five cents. I had
$20.40 in my pocket and no idea how to get to a
Confederate train station. I arrived at the Rayburn house shortly after one in the afternoon.
It was a three-story brick house in a row of
identical houses. The thatch mat in front of the
door was the only thing that separated it from
the houses around it. A man in a dark suit
answered the door. "May I help you?"

"Yes, I'm here to see the Richard Rayburn
family."

"This is the Rayburn residence," he said holding the door only halfway open.

"Are you Mr. Rayburn?"

The muscles around his lips tightened as he
suppressed a smile. "No, ma'am. I'm the butler."

"How do you do." I put out my hand. "I'm
Edith, Edith Shay." It was not the time to come
clean with my real name.

Meeting a butler was a highlight for me. I had
heard about them, read about them in books, but
I'd never met one. It was like having a fictional
character become real.

He shook my hand with an amused smile on
his face. "Good to meet you, ma'am. My name is
Gregory Bishop."

"Nice to meet you. May I come in?"

"Certainly." He stepped aside to show me into the foyer. "I'll tell Mrs. Rayburn you're here, but first allow me to take your packages."

Mrs. Richard Rayburn carried more fabric than skin. Her dress was so full, no one could get within five feet of her. Her hair stood several feet over her head, all piled up in fancy, stiff black curls that didn't so much as jiggle when she walked. She brought me into the parlor. Mr. Bishop followed with the packages. She told him to put them down in the corner, then offered me tea. It was brought in by a maid. Mrs. Rayburn's conversation was so trivial I can't remember a word she said.

The walls around us were painted white, and they reflected the sunlight from the windows to a blinding degree. It was several minutes before my eyes adjusted to the room and I was able to look around.

I knew from Doreen Rayburn that her son had five children. The parlor I sat in wasn't the parlor of a family with five children. The tables were dusted to a polish and decorated with fine glass figurines. The floor was covered with a knobby white rug. The settee I was seated on was as white as the dots under my fingernails. There was no room for children in that parlor.

"When do the children come home?"

My abrupt question shocked Mrs. Rayburn. It made it quite obvious that I hadn't heard a word she was saying. She shifted in her chair and replied, "Gregory brings them home at four."

I couldn't imagine spending three hours in that room with Mrs. Rayburn, so I suggested, "Shall I leave the presents with you?"

"Oh." She looked at the pile of packages in the corner as if she had forgotten about them. "If you wish. I don't for the life of me know why she continues to send them. She has this absurd idea that our children are still babies. She buys them tops and little wheeled toys when my youngest is eleven years of age. He plays piano, not jacks."

"Hasn't she seen them?"

"No." She turned away. "Doreen is a stubborn old woman. She refuses to come to Washington. She'd rather wither away in that old house."

"You don't visit her?"

"Not that it is any of your business, Miss Shay, but that's a flight of fancy. I can't get my children to walk to school together, let alone take them hundreds of miles by train. Besides, Richard is far too busy at the university to leave."

I nodded, but inside I was planning to kidnap the children and take them to Philadelphia. Their mother was a nightmare. She wore enough face powder to resemble whitewashed bricks. She filled her house with useless trinkets and talked about her children as if they were things, not people. I had to stay to be sure the children received the presents.

The mother's effect on them was obvious from the moment they walked in the door. Their clothing was unwrinkled and totally unfitting for anyone below the age of twenty. The two boys were wearing woolen suits complete with starched collars and ties. The two girls wore knee-length dresses and wool stockings, but their hair was in finger curls without ribbons. Those poor girls would have had to sit still for at least an hour a day for someone to curl their hair. Each child kissed their mother on the cheek, bowed in greeting, then ran from the room. Mrs. Rayburn never said a word about the gifts.

When we were alone again, I asked, "You have a fifth child?"

"Yes, Amelia." For the first time, I saw Mrs. Rayburn smile with genuine emotion. It creased her face from her eyes to her chin. "She's attending the university where her father works. She studies women's sciences."

"Women's sciences?"

"Yes, all the proper ways to cook, clean, and raise children."

I couldn't see how those things could be taught in a classroom, but I was fascinated by the opportunity to meet a woman who was going to college—a woman close to my age, no less. Amelia was the reason I stayed until supper. She arrived just as the meal was being served. She went straight to kiss her father, who was seated at the head of the table reading a newspaper.

"Evening, Mother." She bowed to her mother, then sat down.

"You're late." Her mother kept smiling through her anger.

"Sorry, Mother. Professor Nelson's cooking lecture ran long this afternoon."

Richard Rayburn introduced me as his mother's cook, then no one referred to me again. I enjoyed the meal, but I felt like I was more a part of the furniture than a guest in their house. I thought of mentioning the gifts, but no one talked after the main course was served, so I was afraid to speak. When the meal was finished, I was about to ask if I could see the children open their gifts before I left, but Mrs. Rayburn cut me off by shouting to her husband, "Richard, this poor dear has come a great distance. Shouldn't we put her up for the night?"

"Certainly." Richard smiled. "You can have the guest room, Edith."

"Harriet, show Miss Shay the guest room," Mrs. Rayburn told the maid.

I was rushed off before I could say more than thank you. The room was the same size as the first floor of my house. I could actually lose my breath running from one end to the other, which I did, but of course the corset was a definite disadvantage. I lay down crossways on the bed and my feet didn't hang over the edge. For the first time, I could see myself snuggled into a bed that size with my husband and all our children—the elbows and cold feet, wiggling bodies, and laughing faces—it would be wonderful.

A knock at the door pulled me out of the dream. "Who is it?"

"It's Amelia."

I sat up to say, "Come in."

Amelia slid into the room, then leaned against the wall by the door. "I'm not disturbing you, am I?"

"No."

"I was just wondering if you could tell me about Grandma Rayburn."

"You haven't met her?"

"Certainly, but I haven't seen her in years." Amelia came forward. I motioned for her to take a seat next to me on the bed, and she did. "Mother thinks she's too old-fashioned. She hates the things Grandma gives us, says they're working-class things."

"I didn't see her wrap them."

"I won't see them either. Mother throws them out."

In a flash, I was mad enough to set Mrs. Richard Rayburn's dress on fire. "That's unconscionable."

Amelia closed her eyes and shook her head as she waved her hand in the air, saying, "I don't even want to think about my mother. Tell me about Grandmother."

"Your grandmother is wonderful. She's the best cook I've ever met."

"Going to college was the only way I could learn to cook."

"What is college like?"

"Well, that depends on if you're a man or a woman." Amelia sighed. "My classes are practical lessons about cooking and cleaning, but sometimes I sneak into the bigger auditoriums after class has started and sit on the floor. No one can see me, and I hear every word. Men have all the luck. Their classes can be about anything from the history of this country to the composition of the human brain."

"Really?"

Amelia turned to face me and leaned forward to explain. She recited what she remembered of the lectures she'd heard about a Frenchman named Voltaire who made up ideas about the brain. He said it had tiny pathways by which messages were delivered to tell the body what to do. She talked about a man named Pasteur who discovered tiny little bugs that make food rot. I listened for hours as Amelia described all the things she learned at the university. What she didn't pick up in class, she read in the library, which had so many thousands of books a girl could get lost in the stacks without being noticed. When the light went out under the door, we lay down and continued to talk in whispers. I fell asleep listening to a story about how Voltaire had wanted to rid the world of Bibles only to have his home turned into a Bible press after his death. I wished such a revenge upon Mr. Denison.

As I slept, I dreamed of Doreen Rayburn wrapping packages for the children. She was smiling with tears in her eyes. Her daughter-in-law stormed into the room and ripped the presents right out of Doreen's hands. Doreen tried to get them back, but her daughter-in-law wouldn't let go. The boxes were torn apart and the contents smashed to pieces on the floor.

I woke up in a sweat and knew I had to find the gifts. When I went downstairs, the kitchen light was on. I knew the Rayburns didn't go into their kitchen, so I went in. Harriet was warming something on the stove. "I'm sorry to bother you, miss."

I startled her. She backed away from the stove, saying, "I was making myself a bit of warm milk to help me sleep."

"For my father, it's tea." I smiled.

She nodded. "Can I help you, miss?"

"Yes, do you know what Mrs. Rayburn did with the packages I brought?"

"She burned them."

"She what?"

"She burned them. She always burns things from Mother Rayburn. They're feuding."

"Why?"

"I can't tell you." She shook her head and turned away.

"Please, I won't share a word of it with anyone."

The maid looked from side to side as if she was expecting someone else to be listening, "You'll be leaving tomorrow; I can tell you. Mr. Rayburn paid for Mother Rayburn to come to

Washington. As soon as she walked in the door, Mother Rayburn kept pointing out the things Mrs. Rayburn didn't know how to do. She didn't cook. She didn't knit. She didn't bathe her own children. They had a big argument about nannies and servants. Mother Rayburn got so mad she told Mrs. Rayburn she wasn't a fit mother. No mother would dress her children up like department store dolls, that's what Mother Rayburn said. I heard her clear as a bell from this very room." She pointed at the wet floor.

Doreen's stubborn strength had cost her the right to see her grandchildren. She stood still on that platform because she knew the presents I brought wouldn't ever reach her grandchildren. I wasn't going to let Mrs. Rayburn win. I went back upstairs to get the packages out of the suitcase. As I saw it, Edith had more than likely replaced all the gifts in the seven months since she'd lost her suitcase. I could pay her for the gifts I used, and the children would get presents from their grandmother.

I hadn't so much as looked inside the suitcase since I got it back from Mr. Denison. When I took the packages out, I could see that the sealing wax on each package had been broken and replaced with blue candle wax.

It felt good to tear open the packages and

crush the ridiculous wax Mr. Denison used to cover up his greed. The gifts inside weren't the useless trinkets he had thought they were. Edith had wrapped up parts of her own life. Some of the objects were obviously used, but well aged. I hadn't noticed it before, but the binding of *The English Orphan* was torn. The pocket watch had a winding pin that was silver instead of gold. There was a snuffbox with snuff inside. The one I couldn't put down was a locket which contained two pictures. They were the faces of two women. One was older, my mother's age perhaps, her eyes squinted and her hair pulled tight into a bun on top of her head. The other was a young woman with a smile on her rounded face. Either one of them could have been Edith. I decided to wear it.

The other items were unmarked by use. There was a set of embroidered handkerchiefs, a leatherbound journal with thick, tan pages, an empty picture frame made of pewter turned black with age, a gold watch fob, a set of pearl earrings, a string of blue glass beads, a silver vest button chain with fake coins dangling from its links, a tin pillbox with flowers carved into the cover, a tin of marbles, and a short china doll with wiggly eyes and stiff, chestnut horsehair on its head. I surrounded myself with those tiny treasures.

The birds had begun to sing before I could decide which gift to give to each child. I hid them all in my satchel so that Amelia wouldn't see. When Mr. Rayburn came to my door to take me to Arlington, I insisted upon saying good-bye to the children. They were all lined up in the foyer with snarly hair and droopy eyes when I came downstairs. Mrs. Rayburn was made up and smiling in the doorway to the parlor.

"First, I'd like to thank you both for your hospitality," I said as I looked from Mrs. Rayburn to Mr. Rayburn. They nodded in turn. I clutched the pearl earrings in my hand and moved closer to the children. "Amelia, thanks so much for the talk last night. I'll never forget it." I gave her a hug and she kissed me on the cheek. "This is for you, from your grandmother." I tucked the earrings into her hand. She squealed. I didn't dare look in Mrs. Rayburn's direction, but I could feel the heat of her anger on the back of my neck.

I moved to Amelia's brother Charles, who wore striped pajamas that made him look like a stick of peppermint suck candy. "Do you have a watch?" He nodded. "Then this is yours." I placed the watch fob in his open palm.

The children had formed a half-circle around me waiting for their turns. I gave the blue beads to Elizabeth who had worn a necklace the day before. She put it on as soon as I handed it over. I moved on to Mary, who stood biting her lip with her hand outstretched. I gave her the china doll. She hopped with joy exclaiming, "It's so beautiful. Isn't it beautiful?"

I gave the marbles to the youngest boy who would rather play the piano according to Mrs. Rayburn's account. He dropped to the bottom step to examine them on the spot. When I stepped to the door he was rolling them across the floor.

"My mother has outdone herself this time." Mr. Rayburn smiled. "Children, you'll have to write to her immediately. Gregory will drop your letters off at the post office on your way to school."

There was a chorus of "yes, sirs," and the children started to make their way upstairs. Mary was the first to turn and say, "Thanks for bringing these to us, Miss Shay." The others followed her example, shouting their thanks.

I was ready to cry. Part of me was praying the real Edith could hear them give thanks for her gifts. I also felt a bit guilty for giving away her things. Mrs. Rayburn made it worse. Her face resembled the plaster statue in their front yard. It was drawn into a scowl that could turn a person to stone. I forced a smile. "Thank you again."

• • •

Richard Rayburn took me to the Virginia Railroad Station in Arlington. He thanked me for bringing his mother's gifts and left none the wiser about his wife's cruelty. There was nothing more I could do but be on my way.

It seemed so natural to step onto the train. I relished the rush of excitement as the engine started to pull it away from the station. I knew then I was just where I was supposed to be.

I leaned back in the seat and let my mind wander. Part of me hoped that Edith was the young woman in the locket. It was possible she was a college student like Amelia who could tell me all the things she knew. We'd walk arm in arm across the college campus, the sun on our faces, the trees swaying above us.

"Katherine, many men fear smart women. Proves their theories wrong."

"Excuse me?"

"Oh, men try to believe women are the weaker sex. More emotional, less logical. Unable to think for themselves."

"I worked for a man like that." I felt like spitting on the memory of Mr. Denison. Edith would join me, I'm sure.

"Oh, but you'll find yourself a man who can appreciate a woman who understands how this here world works."

We'd laugh together about the strange things young men do, like the way they shuffle their feet and look at the ground when they're trying to ask a young lady a question. She would be a sister to me. Like the Dyer sisters, we might be married on the same day to brothers. I missed seeing the Dyer sisters. To be truthful, I missed the love they showed each other. The way Opal would pull Rachel's scarf over her nose and announce, "Fit for any storm." They'd laugh. I needed to feel that kind of love.

I relaxed, and a memory drifted into my thoughts. It was a Saturday in March. We'd had an unexpected storm. There were several inches of snow on the ground and the wind was still making the pine trees talk. I insisted on going to the train station with Father, and he didn't protest. Mother couldn't stop fussing. She heated my scarf in the stove for a minute or two before tucking it into my coat. She straightened my collar and buttoned me up. I carried rocks in my pocket that Mother had heated for me. I felt the hot stone surface on my fingertips as I sat in that train.

I'd had that love and walked away. I wanted to show my mother what she really meant to me. I could put it into a letter, but what would I say? Using Mason Rayburn's stationery, I tried to write her a letter. I talked about warmed rocks and corn muffin batter licked from a spoon, the dresses she sewed for me, the Christmas quilt—I rambled on, but it all seemed so unreal, so far away. I didn't have the proper words to say what I really meant. I promised myself I would find a way to tell her when I went back to Wisconsin.

I thought back to my first letter to Aeslynn, but I knew then that the letter I'd sent her was inadequate, too. I should have told her all about Mr. Denison. How if it wasn't for her, I wouldn't have had the strength to face him. Had I met Mr. Denison before her, I would never have made it past Chicago.

Amelia's mother had cheated Doreen Rayburn out of the best gift anyone could have given her, so I wrote to tell her about her grandchildren. I described them from head to foot, from the freckles lining Mary's cheekbones, to the gap between Charles's teeth. I relayed their gratitude for her gifts, then I stopped short. I realized the children would write to her and she'd know they didn't get the gifts she had sent. I faced up to my decision and told her exactly what had happened, from Mrs. Rayburn's destruction of the packages to the substitutions I made from the suitcase.

I tucked the letter into my pocket. I was almost more eager to get that letter in the mail than I was to see Richmond. In fact, I was so anxious that I ran from the train station to the nearest post office two blocks away without so much as taking in the color of the station's walls. It felt good to know that I had sent something to Doreen.

After handing the letter over to the postal official, addressed and stamped, I took a look around. The office was only a single room with a long boxed-in counter with a shield between the postal worker and customers. The rest of the room was bare except for a few flyers glued to the wall. One aged notice caught my eye. It read: "Don't let the Yankees have your land and your pride. Send your valuables to safety. Mail your precious heirlooms to be stored in a post office box in a northern city of your choice. The contents of the box will be kept in the strictest confidence by dedicated postal employees." I rubbed the locket with the knowledge that Edith Shay had been trying to get her family's valuables to safety.

I stepped out onto the boardwalk to take in the city of Richmond. In a moment's glance, I believed that a city could be devoured by war. There were gaps between buildings where destroyed businesses once stood. Bricks, glass, and weeds crowded the empty lots. Many of the windows were boarded up or bricked in. The bank across the street was scarred with smoke stains. The plaster building at the end of the block looked more like marble with the cracks running down its walls. Several of the gargoyles that decorated the roof were missing altogether. Sections of many of the roofs were brand new. Business was still conducted, people still walked the streets, but there was a silence that carried on above all the noise. I imagined that it was a shared memory of the destruction and the death that had delivered the city to the Union army in April of 1865. I went back inside, afraid to open my mouth again.

"Can you direct me to Fillmore Street?"

"Certainly." The postal clerk didn't change his sullen expression. "It's about thirty-seven blocks east of here."

"Can I hire a coach from anywhere nearby?"

"The train station."

"Of course, thank you."

"Welcome."

I kept my eyes on the floor of the coach for what seemed like hours—afraid of what I'd see outside the window. "Nineteen-nineteen Fillmore!" The coachman's muffled voice announced our arrival. I didn't move. He shouted again louder. "Nineteen-nineteen Fillmore!"

I climbed out without looking at the houses on the street. I paid the coachman and he pulled away. Edith Shay's house was right behind me. I could see its shadow reaching over the street, disappearing under the carriages as they passed by. The woman I had dreamed about was inside the house, wondering whatever became of her suitcase.

The house was set back from the road. A felled Wisconsin pine could have bridged the gap between me and the house. It was white, with a porch. The floor was inlaid brick; the support beams were eight-by-eight boards. The front door was solid wood with indented panes painted black. The gray shutters were chipped and closed. There was a row of staggered flag-stones leading to the front door.

I stepped from one stone to another and remembered crossing the Wabash River on the flattened stones left over from a failed dam Great-Grandpa Warren had built to have enough water for his cornfields. I was so nervous I could have held my hand up and let my shaking do the knocking. I lifted my hand up three times, but never touched the door.

It opened and a woman stood in the shadows of the hallway. She wore a floor-length dress not much different from the woolen one I wore. We stared at each other for a moment, waiting for the other to speak. I remember she had a mole on her chin that made me think she'd let a currant berry fall out of her mouth. "Can I help you?"

I opened my mouth and a sigh came out, then I stammered, "I'm looking for Edith Shay."

"Edith Shay?" She repeated the name as if she was reading it in a letter. "Oh, that's Wallis's grand-mother. Honey, the Shays haven't lived here for years. They went north when the Yankees come, all except Edith. She went up to see her kin, but she died. She died in some train station in Michigan last August."

The door closed. Stunned, I stepped into the street. Wandering, I tried to understand what this all meant. Edith Shay dead? Her suitcase left for lost? I'd dragged her suitcase across the country, stolen her name, and she would never know.

She'd probably been laid in her grave before I even reached Chicago. She'd left this earth an old woman holding onto pieces of the life she was leaving behind. I came along hoping to make something out of the life God gave me.

I had thought the train to Chicago would be my chariot to a divine land, but it was really a rail ride into real life—a life where I had to fight for my money with callused hands and my own good sense. I didn't have much else when I went walking into that city.

Seemed like I didn't know much until I left a place. I was too busy working or burying my nose in print to pay attention to the real things happening around me. The horizon was my destination, and there was no one who was going to keep me from flying over it. I'd had no idea how much love and security I'd had in Wisconsin until my parents closed the door in my face. But I knew now, no door closes forever. Hang the consequences. I was starting to gain on myself. My mind was getting quicker. I was seeing things for what they were when they happened.

I stood there staring at the burnt-out shell of a house in front of me, seeing a reflection of myself tilting in a cracked window. I'd shed Katherine Candace Lunden, the small-town Wisconsin girl who looked like she needed a handout, and made my own self. I could stop letting my heart lead me by a string, choose my own destinations. I'd read articles by women who had traveled to this place or that. Why couldn't I do the same thing? Perhaps I could stay in Richmond and write about my travels to Chicago and Philadelphia and Washington. Give a Northerner's view of Richmond. My letter of recommendation from Mr. Denison might even get me into a newspaper office. I could be a travel correspondent—writing the stories I had loved to read as a child. The thought of it made my skin turn to gooseflesh.

I had promised to return to Wisconsin, but I didn't say I would stay for more than a visit. And a visit it would be. I had to keep traveling. But where would I go? New York City? The prairies of Nebraska? The mountains of Montana? Indeed! I was a woman who could make her own way.

I realized as I stood in that muddy Richmond street, Edith Shay died on the bench where I was born. And now it was up to me to set my next course. Nodding, I took Edith's suitcase in hand and made my way back to the train station. There was plenty of country left to see and write about.